Snow on the Roses

Also by John R. Riggs

Killing Frost

Cold Hearts and Gentle People

Dead Letter

A Dragon Lives Forever

The Glory Hound

Haunt of the Nightingale

The Last Laugh

Let Sleeping Dogs Lie

One Man's Poison

Wolf in Sheep's Clothing

SNOW ON THE ROSES

John R. Riggs

A GARTH RYLAND MYSTERY

BARRICADE BOOKS, INC.
NEW YORK

Published by Barricade Books, Inc.
150 Fifth Avenue
New York, NY 10011

Printed in the United States of America.

Book design and page layout by CompuDesign

Library of Congress Cataloging-in-Publication Data

Riggs, John R., 1945–
Snow on the roses / by John R. Riggs.
p. cm. —(A Garth Ryland mystery)
ISBN 1-56980-072-3 (cloth)
1. Ryland, Garth (Fictitious character)-Fiction.
2. Journalists-Wisconsin- Fiction. I. Title.
II. Series: Riggs, John R., 1945–
Garth Ryland mystery.
PS3558.1372S66 1996
813'.54—dc20 95-51078
CIP

First printing

For Aunt Ruth and Denny
and always to Carole

A good knife was never made out of bad steel.

Poor Richard's AlmanacK

CHAPTER 1

You always remember where you were and what you were doing when you heard the bad news. When President Kennedy died, I was on my way back from class at the University of Wisconsin in Madison. My roommate told me as I walked in the door of our room.

I didn't believe it at first, later didn't want to believe it when I saw the riderless black horse, the backward boots in the stirrups, little John-John bravely salute the casket of his father. Only in retrospect have I come to believe it. When I count the years passed. When I measure the distance traveled.

When Grandmother Ryland died, I was managing editor of the *Milwaukee Journal* and living in Brown Deer. I got the phone call at midnight, went to work anyway, ate a brown-bag breakfast, drank a double martini lunch, and only came home because there was nowhere else to go. My infant son had died in September seven months before, and by then my wife and I were just putting in our time, so Grandmother's death leveled me—right down to rock bottom. But there along with the snakes and the spiders, along with the things that I didn't want to face, and the decisions that I didn't want to make, I found my roots, myself again.

After my wife and I were divorced, I quit my job at the *Milwaukee Journal* and used the money that I had inherited from Grandmother Ryland to buy the *Oakalla Reporter,* the same small weekly newspaper in Oakalla, Wisconsin, that I still owned and operated some fifteen years later. Along with the money to buy the *Oakalla Reporter,* I also inherited Grandmother's eighty-acre farm, her brown Chevy sedan aptly named Jezebel, and most of the values that I tried to live by. But there were times, like today, that I wished that she had been less earthbound, less rooted in this mortal, temporal life, less tenacious in her love and in her grief.

"Garth. . ."

"Abby, what's wrong?"

When the phone rang that Thursday morning, I was in my office, writing my column for that week's *Oakalla Reporter.*

"It's Doc. He's dead." She couldn't hide the tremor in her voice.

"You're sure?" I asked, refusing to believe it.

"Garth, I'm a doctor. Remember?"

"I'll be right there."

Outside, I shoved my hands into the pockets of my jacket and started walking up Gas Line Road. The sun, blurred by a strand of clouds, was just up and at my back. The wind, sharp for early October, was out of the northeast and with a winter sweep to it. The first killing frost of the season still blanketed the roofs and yards the way it had on my way to work. Most everywhere I looked, I could see color in the trees.

Ben Bryan, the county coroner, pulled up beside me in his tan Oldsmobile Eighty-eight. "Need a ride?" he said.

A small, salty man with short grey hair and a love of classic cars, Ben Bryan was a retired mortician who had become county coroner by default a few years ago when no one else would take the job. Now approaching seventy-five, he would gladly have given it up to the first comer, but so far no one but Dr. Abby Airhart had shown an interest. Ben was training Abby for the job, if and/or when she decided that she wanted it.

"You going to Doc's?" I asked.

"Yes. Abby called me right after she called you."

"Then I might as well ride along."

Doc Airhart lived, as he had for the past fifty-five years, in a big white house with a big stone porch right at the Y of Madison Road and Fickle Road, and directly across the street from the United Methodist Church. Formerly Cuyahoga County, Ohio, coroner and at one time ranked among the top surgeons in the world, William T. Airhart was the closest thing to an icon that we had in Oakalla. He had known most of us all of our lives, saved many of our lives at one time or another, and helped keep the rest of us going, so when he retired fifteen years ago at age seventy-five, the whole town, including me, turned out to pay our respects. I merely idolized him then. Since, I had come to love him.

Ben Bryan pulled into Doc's drive and turned off the Oldsmobile. He sat for a moment then said, "I don't want to go in there."

"That makes two of us."

"I thought the old fart would live forever, hoped he would anyway."

The best I could do was nod.

Abby met us at the door and was in my arms before either of us had to think about it. Neither of us was doing very well. Neither was Ben Bryan, who stepped to one side and turned his back to us.

"Where is he?" I finally asked.

"In his bedroom."

"In bed?"

"Yes. He died in his sleep."

Thank God for small favors.

We went on inside the house where I could hear Doc's English setter, Daisy, barking and scratching at the basement door, wanting into the kitchen. Daisy was a present from me to Doc after his old setter, Belle, had died a couple years ago. Daisy was that rarest of birds in either dogs or men, a natural. Just last Saturday, in her first official hunt, she had pointed more grouse than Doc and I had seen in total the past two years. Doc remarked on our way home that if she kept that up, he might have to start buying shells for his gun.

"Have you told Daisy yet?" I asked Abby.

"I'm leaving that up to you."

Abby and Ben waited in the living room while I went on down the hall to Doc's bedroom. There I stood at the threshold a moment before I went inside. Nothing remarkable about the room. White plaster walls, a white pine floor, a chestnut bed and matching chestnut chest of drawers, and nearly matching chestnut dresser. A five-by-seven of Doc's late wife, Constance, standing at one end of the dresser, a five-by-seven of Doc and a very young Belle at the other end. Dust on the photographs and the dresser itself. A pair of folded white wool socks lying on the floor beneath the chest of drawers.

The only remarkable thing was the man lying there in his red silk pajamas, his eyes closed, the hint of a smile on his face, his thatch of snow-white hair as unruly as ever. He couldn't know how much I already missed him and probably wouldn't have approved when I leaned down to kiss him.

When I came out of the bedroom, Ben Bryan went in. Abby and I went to the kitchen to drink a cup of coffee. As I glanced at the clock on the wall, I saw that it was only 8 A.M. That left a lot of day to fill.

"So, what's your verdict?" Abby asked, as she handed me a cup of coffee, then sat down at the kitchen table across from me.

As usual, the kitchen smelled like apples. As usual, the black overhead fan (stilled now for winter) hung from a yellow ceiling over a burnt-red linoleum floor. And as usual, the sight of Dr. Abby Airhart, niece of the late William T. Airhart, brought out the best in me. Bright eyed and fair skinned, with soft, thick hair the color of wheat straw and a smile that went to her soul, Abby Airhart was the surgeon at the Adams County Hospital and the new darling of Oakalla's citizens, young and old alike. Today, however, wearing a frayed white cotton robe, and the face of little-girl-lost, she hardly looked the part.

"What do you mean, what's my verdict?" I said. "I thought you said he died in his sleep?"

"He did." She took the time to light a cigarette. "I think."

I waited while she took a drag on her cigarette. A non-smoker all of my life, I found it ironic that, as I approached the big 50, when we all are supposedly getting smarter, I would fall in love with a smoker for the first time in my life. A surgeon at that, and fifteen years my junior. I guessed that if you lived long enough, life was full of surprises.

"Explain yourself, please," I said.

"There's nothing to explain. . . I guess."

"Damn it, Abby. Is there or isn't there?"

She shrugged, gave me a helpless look. She hadn't yet touched her coffee, and I hadn't yet touched mine.

"I don't know, Garth. He seemed fine when he went to bed. It's just hard to believe. . ." She stopped as tears came into her eyes. "That he died. So suddenly, I mean. Without even a good-bye."

"Yeah, I know," I said. "I feel the same way."

"But he did have a bad heart."

"Agreed."

During our Saturday grouse hunt, Doc had stopped several times to rest and once to pop a couple nitroglycerin pills before he went on. Though concerned, I hadn't thought much about it since it had happened before.

"And when you have a bad heart, and you're ninety, you can go at any time," she said. "Even if you *are* Doc Airhart."

Daisy took the silence that followed as her cue to resume whining and scratching at the basement door. I was tempted to get up and let her out, but I knew that the first thing that she would do would be to make a beeline for Doc's bedroom. Neither Abby nor I was prepared for that.

Meanwhile Ben Bryan came into the kitchen to call Operation Lifeline, our local ambulance service. Though it had improved over the years that I had known it, particularly since Abby's arrival, Operation Lifeline still did not have a flawless reputation among the citizenry of Oakalla. Rupert Roberts, former sheriff of Adams County, once compared a ride in it to a roll at the crap table, and Ruth, my housekeeper, refused to ride in it under any circumstance, even death. Still, I doubted that today Doc would mind.

"You want an autopsy?" Ben asked Abby.

"I don't know. What do you think?"

"You're the doctor."

"What would Doc do?" she said.

"Is there any reason to believe that it was anything but a natural death?"

She hesitated a moment then said, "No."

"Then I wouldn't bother," Ben said."You need a ride anywhere, Garth?"

After thinking it over, I said, "No."

"Then I'll be going as soon as Operation Lifeline gets here. Where do you want them to take Doc's body?"

Abby looked at me, but I didn't have an answer for her. "The hospital, I guess," she said. "Until I decide what to do with him."

I studied her. There was something that she wasn't telling me, but I had no idea what. "Abby, are you sure that's wise?" Once Doc was at the hospital, if Abby had any doubts at all, she might be tempted to cut him open.

"Probably not" was all she said.

"If you're not completely sure, why don't you send him home with me for now?" Ben offered.

"I hate to impose."

"It's no imposition. Doc and I go back a long ways."

Operation Lifeline soon came and took Doc away. Ben Bryan left with them, leaving Abby and me alone in the house. Except for Daisy's pitiful whine, it was quieter in there than I ever remembered.

"So. . . ," Abby said, slapping her hands down on the table. "Where do we go now?"

"Back to work, I guess. I have a deadline to meet."

"And I. . ." She glanced at the clock. ". . . have to be in surgery within the hour."

"No rest for the wicked."

"It seems not." She was distant, almost cold, and not at all the Abby that I had come to know and love.

"Why did you hesitate when Ben asked you where to take Doc's body? Didn't you ever discuss with him what he wanted done with it?"

She said, "We discussed it. But I'm about to overrule him."

"What do you mean?"

She took a deep breath then slowly let it out. "Because, damn him, he wanted to donate his body to science, and I'm not going to let that happen." She closed her eyes, but the tears won out. "I'm just not going to let that happen. They're going to have to find somebody else to practice on."

"Doc's not going to like that."

"That's his problem." She opened her eyes, which glistened with tears and fire. "And yours, if you don't agree with me."

"I'm not taking sides. Just trying to be fair."

"Could *you* send him off somewhere to be sectioned like a slab of beef into all his separate parts?"

"No. But aren't you glad that someone somewhere sometime did?"

"Don't be logical. I'm not in the mood for it."

Or for anything else, it seemed like.

"I'd better go," I said, rising from the table. "Are you going to be all right?"

She shook her head no. "Probably not for a long time."

"But you can still operate?"

"Can you still print a newspaper?"

"Touché." I emptied my nearly full coffee cup into the sink. "Speaking of which, do you happen to know where Doc keeps his memoirs?"

After several years of asking and for several weeks

running now, I had been printing Doc's memoirs in the *Oakalla Reporter.* For spite, he usually delivered them to me late on Thursday for Friday's edition. He only did it that way because he knew that (1) I owed him too many favors to protest and (2) "Doc Remembers" was the most popular series ever to be featured in the *Oakalla Reporter.* Thanks to him, I could almost afford the new press that I had been wanting for years.

"In his office, I think. At least that's where he wrote most of the time."

"Do you mind if I look for them?"

"No. Why should I? Life goes on, right?"

"I loved him, too, Abby. Don't forget that."

"As he loved you. I'm sorry, Garth. I'm not tracking very well right now." She rose from the table but left her coffee sitting there. "Feel free to look around. I've got to get ready."

"I'll give you a holler before I leave."

She forced a smile. "See that you do."

Doc's office, which was past his bedroom and all the way to the end of the hall, was the former waiting room of his medical office. It used to have an outside door, a black-and-white tile floor, venetian blinds on its two tall windows, and several straight-backed wooden chairs that sat like rocks, yet always seemed to be filled, a tall wooden coatrack that also always seemed to be filled, and always everywhere, coming from the pores of the room itself, the smell of camphor and alcohol.

Doc had since paneled the walls and taken out the door, ripped up the tile and plywood and gone down to the original pine plank floor, added bookshelves and memorabilia, including his first scalpel and stethoscope, then set a big oak desk and chair right in the middle of the room. But the smell of camphor and alcohol still lingered. As did the memories.

Doc's memoirs weren't there in his office. I determined that after searching through the mile-high stack of books and papers on his desk and going through all of his desk drawers. Thinking that in my haste to find them I might have missed them, I repeated my search but with the same results.

"Any luck?" Abby asked me a few minutes later. Wearing grey slacks and a neon-green windbreaker, she was on her way out the door.

"No. I can't find them anywhere."

"You look in his bedroom?"

"Yes. They weren't there either."

"Well, I'll look tonight when I get home." She glanced vacantly around the house. "It will give me something to do."

"Do you want company?"

"You have a deadline to meet. Remember?"

"After it's met?"

"No. I'll be fine. Really." She took a long look down the hall that led to Doc's office, shuddered, tried not to let me see it. "I've got to run."

But I caught her arm before she could leave. "Abby, what aren't you telling me?"

"About what?"

"Anything."

"It's nothing, Garth, really," she said as she pulled her arm free.

"Why don't you tell me anyway." I wasn't asking.

She shrugged as if to make light of it. "Just a dream I had. A nightmare really. That Daisy was barking and someone was in the house."

"Last night?"

"Yes. It woke me up."

"Was Daisy still barking?"

"No. It was all quiet by then. But that's why when I awakened this morning and Uncle Bill wasn't up yet as he usually is, I went to his bedroom to check on him."

"And found him dead."

"Yes. Found him dead."

"With a pair of clean socks on the floor."

She stared at me, not quite understanding, nor not wanting to. "It was just a dream, Garth. No one was there."

"Were your doors locked?"

"The front one was. The back one wasn't." Her look said that I should know if anyone should, since I was the main reason why she kept the back door unlocked. "Just like they always are."

"Maybe it wasn't a dream, Abby."

"How are we ever going to know?"

"We can always ask Daisy."

Her eyes grew large as she said, "I already did."

"And what did she say?"

"Woof, woof." She gave me a hurried kiss and left.

CHAPTER 2

I didn't go directly back to my office as I'd planned to do. Instead, I went home first.

"If you're looking for a late breakfast, you're out of luck," Ruth said.

Ruth Krammes, my housekeeper, still sat at the kitchen table where I had left her two hours before. She still wore the ratty pink housecoat that had survived more washings than Miami drug money and the fur-lined moccasins that I had given her several Christmases ago. A big-boned, iron-willed Swede somewhere in her seventies, Ruth had been my housekeeper ever since I bought the *Oakalla Reporter* and moved to Oakalla. Now I didn't know what I would do without her, but there were days, particularly early on in our past, when I would have been willing to try.

"I'm not looking for something to eat," I said, taking my usual seat across the kitchen table from her.

"Then what are you doing home?"

"Doc Airhart died in the night. I thought you'd like to know."

"So that's what the ambulance was doing there."

I should have known that she would already know. Ruth, her cronies, and her many relatives scattered about Wisconsin had a communications network that was second to none.

"So you have moved after all," I said.

"Only to answer the phone."

That said, we sat in silence for a while.

"How's Abby doing?" Ruth finally asked.

"Not well. She seems really angry about it. About something anyway."

"That's to be expected."

"Hell, Ruth, he was ninety years old. What's there to be angry about?"

"Being suddenly alone."

"She has me."

Ruth took a drink of her coffee that had been cold two hours ago. "Such as you are."

"Thanks for the vote of confidence."

"What I mean, Garth, is that you're not her Uncle Bill. She hasn't been coming home to you for the past year. You're not the first one she sees in the morning or the last one she sees at night. . ." She paused momentarily to let me know that she knew what was up. "Not usually anyway. And you don't have to come home to an empty house from now on like she does."

"It's not my fault that he died. At least that's the way she acts, like I'm to blame for something."

"Then maybe there's more to it."

"Such as?"

"Think about it, Garth."

I thought about it, remembered Abby's question, So where do we go from here?

"I get it," I said. "Everything changes now that Doc's dead. You, Abby, and I are now a trio whether we like it or not."

Ruth's look was one I couldn't read, somewhere between sadness and resignation. "Something will have to give, Garth. Eventually. Nothing stays the same forever."

"But why worry about it now, before it happens? That seems pointless somehow."

"I'm not worried about it. I'm not sure Abby is either. But it's not something that any of us can ignore. None of us are getting any younger."

"What's that supposed to mean?"

"Just what I said. If you and Abby are going to have a life together, the time to start is now."

I rose from the table and got me a drink of water. One day at a time was how I learned to survive that time in my life that did not seem survivable. One day at a time it would be now.

"Will you be home for lunch?" Ruth asked.

"Probably not. Supper either, since I still have to write my column and find a replacement for Doc's memoirs."

"Abby won't let you print them now?" She was ready to take issue.

"No. We can't find them."

Ruth seemed to take the news hard. For someone who disdained the past, she took an uncanny interest in it and had an unparalleled memory of it.

"It would be a shame if they stayed missing. That's the best thing you ever did, Garth, talking Doc into publishing them."

"Tell me about it."

"Outside of some of your own writing."

I had to smile. Getting a compliment from Ruth was harder than getting an audience with the pope.

"Thanks for that much anyway," I said.

"You have any idea where Doc's memoirs might be?" Her brows rose ever so slightly, the way they always did when something piqued her curiosity.

"Your guess is as good as mine, Ruth. Unless Doc handed them over to somebody to get a second opinion."

"A second opinion about what, and why would he need one?"

"About what, I can't say. But you know Doc. He always liked to get his facts straight."

Ruth thought a moment, then said, grudgingly it seemed, "Aunt Emma."

"Of course."

Ruth's Aunt Emma lived on Berry Street in the east end of Oakalla a block north of the *Oakalla Reporter*. Hers was a russet two-story frame house, surrounded by conifers and hardwoods, mostly oak, whose now rust-red leaves would hang clustered in the trees until spring, and along with the firs, which would bend with the snow and gather in around the house, at least give the house the appearance of warmth throughout the long winter ahead.

I climbed up onto Aunt Emma's front porch, knocked on her front door, waited a couple minutes, then knocked again. Aunt Emma was a retired army nurse who had been on every continent except Antarctica at least twice and who had served throughout World War II and Korea, and part of Vietnam. In age and spirit, she was the closest thing to a contemporary that Doc Airhart had in Oakalla. An alcoholic, who disappointed her doctor yearly by ignoring his advice and then living to tell him about it, she was also a storehouse of knowledge and Ruth's chief ally or adversary, depending on who was doing the talking, or taking the credit, as was usually the case.

I knocked a third time and was about to give up when Aunt Emma came to the door. Today, as she often did, she wore jeans, a long-sleeve, red-and-white plaid cotton shirt, no shoes, and a scowl on her face.

"Hell, I might have known it was you," she said as she threw open the door to let me in.

"I can't stay," I said, as I stepped inside.

"You never do. You just take what you came for and leave. Like the rest of the men in my life," she muttered while closing the door.

We went into her living room where we sat on her prickly green couch, she at one end and me at the other. I faced the prickly green overstuffed chair that matched the couch. Her right arm rested against an end table on which stood a fat mauve lamp and a glass of scotch. Glenfiddich, I guessed. Aunt Emma could afford the best.

A rocker had been pulled up right against her south window where she would have the best light for reading. A coffee table stood on a purple-and-peach braided throw rug with a carnival-glass dish filled with burnt candy peanuts sitting on top of it. They looked like the same peanuts from my last visit, which was sometime during the summer.

Still, I helped myself to a handful of them. Who knew when lunch would be?

"Those peanuts stale yet?" she said.

I used my finger to pry one off my gum. "Not by more than a year."

"Serves you right. You should come more often."

I nodded, didn't say anything.

"So spit it out," she said. "Say what you came for. My scotch is getting warm."

"Your scotch is always warm." Like Doc Airhart, Aunt Emma drank her scotch straight up, and pity the man who didn't do the same.

"Warm-er, then," she said, correcting herself.

"I came about Doc Airhart. You know he died in the night?"

"I heard" was her answer.

"And his memoirs seem to be missing."

"So?" Aunt Emma crossed her legs and reached for her scotch. As usual, she wouldn't make it easy for me.

"So I was wondering if you had them?"

She took a drink of scotch and set her glass back down. "Why would I have them? They're not my memoirs."

"I thought perhaps he might have wanted your opinion on them."

Aunt Emma was neither as tall nor as broad as Ruth, as the booze kept her shadow thin. But she could muster Ruth's strength when needed and be every bit as stubborn.

"Why would he want my opinion now? He never did before. Not in the fifty-odd years I knew him did that man ever ask me my opinion on anything. He was too busy handing out his own."

"Then that wasn't his Cadillac that I saw parked in front of your house a couple days ago?"

Aunt Emma had hawklike eyes. When she turned up the voltage, she could see right through you.

"Since when did my business become yours?" she said.

"Give me a break, Aunt Emma. Doc's Cadillac is a mile long and a block wide, and he always parks it halfway into the street. How could I miss it?"

"You stayed on the job like you should, you would have."

I stood and made my way to the door. Whether it was the booze or the phase of the moon, this was one of those days that I wasn't going to get anywhere with her.

"Where are you going?" she demanded.

"To work. Where my nose won't be in your business."

"Thin skinned today, aren't we? You'd have never made it in the army, Garth. Taking shit was an occupational hazard."

I nodded then stepped outside. I was thinking that it was one of the hazards of my business, too. Had for a long time now.

At work I began to lay out tomorrow's *Oakalla Reporter* to see what I could use to fill in for Doc's missing memoirs. Usually they took up a full page, so unless I shortened the paper by a page, I had a lot of filling in to do. Except shortening the paper by a page would in effect mean shortening it by two pages from eight to six, since by necessity I had to come out even. I decided to shorten it. Even with Eugene Yuill's long list of speeding tickets, I didn't have a lot of news this week.

That done, I returned to the column that I had been writing when Abby called that morning. What I wanted to say was that the small farmer, like the small town, was in danger of extinction in this country through no fault of his own. As evidence, I offered corn prices forty years ago compared with corn prices today and used my own small farm as an example. The week before, my renter had picked and sold our six thousand bushels of corn at $2 a bushel. Before expenses, which I overlooked for simplicity's sake, he got $6,000 and I got $6,000.

Forty years ago, at just half that yield, that same corn (at $1.50 a bushel, which it was then) would have earned us $2,250 each. Now, here came the rub. Today my $6,000 would buy me a car frame, four tires, and an engine, but not much else under 100,000 miles, unless I wanted something I could pack on my back; or my next year's health insurance premium; or ten tons of potatoes; or 1,000 T-bone steaks. With my corn money forty years ago, I could have blown it all on a '52 Caddy or a '53 DeSoto or a cabin on Buffalo Lake. Or I could have bought a nearly new '54 Chevy Bel Air (perhaps even Jessie's stepmother), along with ten tons of potatoes, 570 T-bone steaks, and (this seemed too good to be true) a full-meal deal from Blue Cross–Blue Shield for $3.06 a month, $4.96 a month if I wanted to count Ruth as family, which I did. And if anyone doubted my statistics, I referred him to the October 1954 issues of the *Madison Capital Times* where I had gotten my information.

So who was kidding whom? Whoever thought that farmers were getting the same slice of the pie, no matter who was doing the cutting, hadn't bought any cornflakes lately.

Once I had said that, I was about to start filling in the rest of the cracks when the phone rang. "Garth, this is Beulah Peters. You haven't seen that sorry excuse we have for a deputy around lately, have you?"

The sorry excuse that we had for a deputy was

Eugene Yuill, a former feed-truck driver and the owner of a pair of size fourteen Redwing work boots, which he wore with regularity both summer and winter. Beulah Peters was a personal nemesis of mine who lived across the street from the school. Along with Doc Airhart, she had the distinction of owning the largest Cadillac in Oakalla.

"What's the problem, Beulah?"

"Well, every day about this time, he's parked in front of my house, looking for speeders. Now, today when I need him, he's not there."

I knew better than to ask, but I asked anyway. Blame it on my low blood sugar. "Why do you need him?"

"Because there's a dog in heat in my front yard, and one of her gentleman callers, a Great Dane by the looks of him, has got himself. . ." Here she paused. "Let's just say in a compromising position. School will be letting out in a few minutes, and I don't think it's something the children should see."

I contemplated the scene for a moment before I said, "I don't think any lives are going to be ruined by that, Beulah. Not in the present day and age."

"Well, it's disgusting if you ask me."

"Then go pour a bucket of cold water on them. I hear that works."

"It might prove traumatic."

"That's the chance you take, Beulah, when you interfere with nature." I hung up and assumed that she did likewise.

A moment later Peanut Johnstone called. Peanut Johnstone ran the Oakalla Telephone Company and doubled as jailer, since the jail was just across the alley from his office.

"Garth, you haven't seen Deputy Yuill anywhere, have you?"

"Not since yesterday. Why?"

"He was supposed to take a prisoner up to Phillips this morning. The prisoner's still here."

"Have you called around, trying to find him?"

"Yes. No one's seen him today."

"Shit," I said, cursing my bad luck and former Sheriff Harold Clark in the same breath. "I don't know where he is, Peanut. Maybe one of his speeders took out a contract on him."

"He has been writing a lot of tickets lately."

"I'll check his house on my way to supper. Maybe he's gone into hiding again for one reason or another."

"I'd appreciate it, Garth. I'm getting tired of feeding this guy."

For want of a nail, I thought as I hung up the phone. If Rupert Roberts hadn't retired, then Harold Clark (Clarkie as he was known in and about Oakalla) would never have become sheriff. If Clarkie had never become sheriff, then Eugene Yuill would never have become his deputy. If Eugene Yuill hadn't become deputy, then Oakalla and I wouldn't have been stuck with him when Clarkie quit earlier this year to take a desk job as a computer jock with the Madison Police Department. And with the sheriff's election only a month away, Eugene Yuill wouldn't have been writing traffic tickets like crazy in order to impress the new sheriff that he was worthy of staying on as deputy. Except, I couldn't figure out why Eugene was trying so hard to hold on to his job. From his first night alone in his patrol car, he had feared his job more than he had loved it, and while it no longer terrified him as it once had, he still couldn't patrol at night without a beer under his belt and his night stick in his lap.

So where was he now? At home, I hoped, nursing a cold.

CHAPTER 3

Not at home, I determined, after rattling his windows and bruising a knuckle on his door. A bachelor now in his fifties, Eugene Yuill lived along Gas Line Road in a small brown shingle-sided house that used to be the office of old Doc Cook, Oakalla's longtime veterinarian, which Eugene had rented for at least the past fifteen years, ever since I had been walking Gas Line Road to work. The house had a living room, bedroom, bathroom, and broom closet, which didn't leave Eugene many places to hide. But from the outside, the house appeared empty even though Eugene's patrol car was parked in his drive. Strange, I thought. Eugene didn't usually hole up until dark.

From there I went to the Corner Bar and Grill where I ordered a fish sandwich, coleslaw, and a Dr. Pepper. I would have rather ordered a Leinenkugel's with my fish sandwich, but on an empty stomach that would have left me somewhere between giddy and somnambulant, neither of which I wanted to be.

As I looked around the barroom, I noticed several of the faithful there, including Dub Bennett, Sniffy Smith, Howdy Heavin, Dewey Clinton, Pete Nelson, and Milo Thomas. And as usual, Dub Bennett was giving Dewey Clinton a hard time.

"Nineteen sixty-two," Dub said to Dewey. "Isn't that the year you said you found the body?"

"Did find it," Dewey insisted, puffing out his chest. "Found two of them."

Dub Bennett, who had turned seventy on his last birthday, was, as in the song "Big John," a big, big man—somewhere around six-four with shoulders that would barely fit through most door frames. He had thin white hair, a calm easygoing presence (unless you got him riled), and a knack for knowing which nerve to hit whenever he wanted to get your goat.

Dewey Clinton was also a big man with a fine head of curly black hair and a smooth, untroubled face that made him look several years younger than I, even though we were about the same age. But despite his size, his bright deep blue eyes that seemed to burn at an inner depth no one, including Dewey, could reach, Dewey was no match for Dub Bennett in either wit or stature.

Dewey was retarded and had been since birth. With his parents dead and no one but his cats for company at home, he usually could be found hanging out somewhere around town—often outside Heavin's Market now that Howdy Heavin had taken over there, and once the market closed, inside the Corner Bar and Grill. In summer, Dewey went shirtless and shoeless, wearing only bib overalls, as his skin turned a dark copper that was the envy of all of us insiders; in winter, fall, and early spring, he wore a sweatshirt under his bib overalls, high-top work shoes with no socks, and if the weather turned really cold, a black wool stocking cap.

"Sure, Dewey," Sniffy Smith said. "You found that body just like the time you found Santa Claus stuck in your chimney."

Sniffy Smith was my barber, who only cut hair on Fridays now that he was retired, and not even then if he didn't feel like it. A small, soft, sad man, Sniffy could either be found at the Marathon Service Station where he spent most of his days or the Corner Bar and Grill where he spent most of his nights. If you found him at home, he was either sick or asleep.

"I did find it!" Dewey bellowed. "Just ask Doc Airhart!"

At the mention of Doc's name, the barroom of the Corner Bar and Grill grew very quiet. I could feel at least a half-dozen pairs of eyes on me. Everybody in there, except perhaps for Dewey Clinton, knew how I felt about Doc.

"Shut up, Dewey," Howdy Heavin said quietly. "I already told you about Doc."

Dewey hung his head. "I'm sorry, Howdy. I forgot."

"Hiram, what do we owe you?" Howdy asked the bartender. "Dewey and I will be leaving now."

Howdy threw a five-dollar bill on the bar and left by the side door. With a look of near panic on his face, Dewey upset his bar stool in his hurry to catch up to him.

"The odd couple," Dub Bennett said as he righted Dewey's stool.

Of Mice and Men, I thought as Hiram set my fish sandwich and coleslaw down in front of me.

Howdy Heavin, after a distinguished twenty-five-year career in the air force, had retired with the rank of major and returned to Oakalla this past summer to help his folks run their market. Though a head shorter than Dewey, and a few years younger, and as sharp as Dewey was dull, he resembled Dewey in at least one respect—his loneliness. Though I liked the man to talk to him, admired his work ethic and his track record, I just couldn't warm up to him. Apparently, except for Dewey Clinton, neither could anyone else in Oakalla.

Sniffy Smith moved from his place at the bar to where I sat in my favorite corner booth—the one that Abby and I always shared whenever we were in there together. I always sat with my back to the wall where I could see all the rest of the room. Perhaps that was because I liked to observe more than I liked to talk, or perhaps I had been Wild Bill Hickok in another life.

"What was that all about?" I asked Sniffy, who had brought a bottle of Hamms with him.

"What was what all about?"

"That business about Dewey finding a body."

"Ask Dub. He's the one who always carried him high about it. Him and Pete and Milo."

Dub Bennett, Pete Nelson, and Milo Thomas had moved into the back room where a euchre game was now in progress. They were three of the players. I didn't see the fourth.

"Where did 1962 come from?" I asked.

Sniffy took a drink of his Hamms. "That's when Dewey said he found the body."

"I mean why did Dub bring it up?"

Sniffy came out with a loud sniff, which he did whenever he got excited, which was how he got his nickname, and which was why I never brought up the subject of women or politics whenever I was getting a haircut.

"You mean you don't know?" he said.

"If I knew, I wouldn't be asking."

"Doc's memoirs! Nineteen sixty-two is coming out tomorrow."

I concentrated on my fish sandwich and tried not to give anything away. Sniffy and the rest of Oakalla would learn the truth soon enough.

"Tell me more," I said.

"You mean Doc didn't mention it in his memoirs? That's what we've been waiting for all year. Dub and Pete and Milo anyway."

"Why are they so interested?"

"Dub because he's just naturally curious about whatever goes on around here. Pete and Milo because they used to live up at that end of the county where it happened. They've been going on and on about Doc's memoirs."

We were going in circles, but that wasn't unusual when I tried to talk to Sniffy. "Which end of the county is that?"

He gave out another loud sniff, which attracted the attention of Hiram, the bartender, and the other two people left in there. "Northeast. Up around Wildwood Bridge. A man drowned up there in the spring of 1962. Dewey claims he's the one who found the body."

"And you don't remember any of the details?"

"That's what I was counting on you for," Sniffy said, looking suspicious. "You and Doc. Seems like nobody can get his story straight, least of all Pete and Milo."

"What about Dewey Clinton? Is there any chance that he could have found the body?"

Sniffy rose from the table, taking his beer with him. "With Dewey, who knows? I hear he used to live up that way. There in the bend in the road above Wildwood Bridge."

"So it is possible?"

"Anything's possible, Garth."

Sniffy kept edging away from me. He was anxious to

get to the back room so that he wouldn't miss his turn when the euchre game ended.

"This is off the subject," I said, "but have you seen Eugene Yuill at all today?"

Sniffy shook his head. "No. Why? Has he gotten lost again?"

"It appears so."

"Well, he'll turn up. He always does." Then Sniffy stopped at the doorway to the back room. He had come to a conclusion and wanted me to know it. "There ain't going to be any 1962 tomorrow, is there, Garth?"

I finished my supper and reached for my wallet. "You'll have to read the paper to find out."

On my way back to work, I stopped at Eugene Yuill's house to see if he'd come home yet. He hadn't by all appearances. Though his patrol car was still parked in the driveway, there were no lights on in his house, no sounds coming from it. I glanced up at the sky. Moonless and white, it had only a sprinkle of stars showing. Still raw out of the northeast, the wind cut into me as I made my way down Gas Line Road. I didn't like the feel of it.

CHAPTER 4

The next morning I sat at the kitchen table drinking my first cup of coffee since last night and watching the day outside try to decide what it wanted to be, blue or grey. I should have been at my office an hour ago, but I didn't want to have to answer the same question for the one thousandth time of where Doc's memoirs were. Ruth sat across the table from me. We had grunted at each other but still hadn't spoken yet.

At ten last night, I had called Abby to see how she was doing and if she wanted me to stop by later. She said how much later, and when I said I didn't know, she said she'd take a rain check, as it had been a long day and she was about to fall on her face. I lied and said I understood.

Sometime after midnight, my printer and I put the *Oakalla Reporter* to bed, and then he and his wife helped me put the mailing labels on before they loaded the papers into their Pontiac station wagon and drove off to the post office. On my way home, I again stopped at Eugene Yuill's house and again saw no sign of him. While there, I felt that old familiar prickling sensation raise the hairs on my nape. Someone unseen was watching me. And not for the first time that night either.

While sitting in my office proofreading the first *Reporter* off the press, I felt as if someone were reading over my shoulder and glanced up to see who was there. It was then that I thought I glimpsed someone at my west window. But when I went to the window to look outside, I saw no one.

"You taking the day off?" Ruth said. "If so, you're still going to have to get your own breakfast."

Ruth didn't cook on Friday morning except by appointment. She said she deserved at least one day a week off, and I agreed with her.

"I haven't decided yet what I'm going to do today," I said.

"You find Doc's memoirs?"

"No. Aunt Emma said they weren't there at her house. Abby said they weren't there at hers either as far as she could tell."

"Then I suggest you find somewhere to hide out."

"I thought of that." I took a drink of my coffee and wished that life always tasted so good. "But Aunt Emma's holding out on me. Or I think she might be."

"It wouldn't be the first time."

While Ruth loved Aunt Emma, professional jealousy kept her from ever admitting it. For a similar reason, I never let Ruth know how much she meant to me. She considered herself indispensable the way it was.

"So what do you think she's keeping from you?" Ruth

asked.

"It's hard to tell. But I saw Doc's Caddy there a couple, three days ago, a fact that she denied, so I'm betting it's something. Doc never was one to waste too many motions."

I could talk about him in the past now, which I couldn't do yesterday. It was a start.

"Maybe she called him about something," Ruth said.

"Maybe. But I doubt it."

I yawned, stretched, and wished for happier times. Even before Doc's death, I had begun to feel Abby pull away from me. Maybe she had already started to read the writing on the wall, to anticipate the changes that Doc's death would bring. I hoped that was all it was anyway.

"A penny for your thoughts," Ruth said.

I shook my head. "I don't have any."

"Rumor has it that Eugene Yuill is missing."

"Rumor has it right."

I got up and poured me a bowl of Honey Nut Cheerios. It was a poor substitute for bacon and eggs, but it would keep the wolf away until lunch.

"So where do you think he is?" she asked.

I added milk, then sat down at the table to eat my cereal. "I have no idea, Ruth. I'll worry about that when I have to."

"I'd be worrying about it right now."

"Why? If it were up to you, Eugene would be tarred and feathered by now."

"I was only going thirty in a twenty when he pulled me over. It cost me half a week's wages."

"He would have let you off with a warning if you'd have kept your mouth shut."

Ruth's face reddened, the way it always did when she knew I had the goods on her. Though Eugene hadn't told me exactly what she'd said to him, the gist of it was that if he had manure for brains, you wouldn't even be able to smell them.

She said, "Be that as it may, the man is missing, and the last time I looked, he was the law in Oakalla."

"Don't remind me."

"So unless you want to start patrolling the streets, I suggest you find Eugene."

"May I eat my breakfast first?"

She folded her arms, looking satisfied. "Be my guest."

My first stop after leaving home was not Eugene Yuill's house but Doc Airhart's. As Abby opened the door, Daisy rushed up to greet me. All whines and wiggles, she wouldn't let me take a step without her being underfoot.

"Where's your ball?" I asked, knowing that it was somewhere around.

She took off for the kitchen and returned carrying a nearly bald tennis ball. I told her to give, she gave it to me, and I made her heel all the way to the back door, where I gave the ball a toss into the backyard. While Daisy chased it down, I closed the door on her.

"That was a dirty trick" Abby said.

"I learned it from your Uncle Bill."

She poured me a cup of coffee, and we sat down at the kitchen table. Twenty-four hours ago, we had been sitting in the same places. But it seemed longer.

Today Abby wore jeans, loafers, and a light-blue chamois shirt, also lipstick and makeup, two things she seldom wore on a workday. Her hair, which came just to her shoulders, looked even softer and thicker than usual.

"Were you expecting someone?" I said.

"Yes. He's here."

"I'm sorry. I had to ask."

She reached across the table and took my hand in

hers. "Don't be sorry. I haven't been myself lately."

"Is there a reason?"

There was. I could see it in her eyes, feel it in the hard knot in my guts.

"As the saying goes, I've been made an offer I can't refuse."

I felt the knot tighten. "Which is?"

"A residency with a doctor I worked with in Detroit. He's chief of pathology at Henry Ford."

"I thought you'd already been through residency?"

"As a surgeon. Not as a pathologist."

"Shit," I said.

"Yeah. That's what I say, too."

She released my hand and leaned back in her chair. I watched the second hand of the clock on the wall take a full turn.

She said, "Of course, it seemed out of the question as long as Uncle Bill was alive because in the first place, he needed me here, and in the second place, he could teach me all that I needed to know about pathology." She smiled, screwed up her courage, said, "Then there's you."

"What about me?" The knot once in my stomach was now up in my throat.

"I love you. Am in love with you. Can't imagine my life without you."

"But. . ." I said because I knew it was coming.

"But outside of you, there's nothing here for me now. What I mean is that while I like my work, and love this town. . ." Tears came into her eyes. "As if it were a part of me. . . I'm not doing what I really want to do, which is to study pathology. In bits and pieces, yes, but not as a whole, not with all of the tools at my command." She angrily swiped at her eyes with the sleeve of her shirt. "Do you understand?"

I glanced down at my cup of coffee that so far had gone begging. Today didn't seem to be starting out any better than yesterday.

"I understand. But that doesn't help me much."

"Either one of us," she said. "But could *you* be anything but what you are?"

"I could be, but I wouldn't be happy at it."

She gave me one of those smiles that you'd walk a mile for. "Not even for me?"

"For you, I'd try."

Her smile faded, became bittersweet. "As I've tried for you."

I glanced down when I heard my heart hit the floor. I had felt worse, but I couldn't remember when.

"So that's it?"

"No. That's not it. I haven't decided yet. I'm just trying to tell you where I am."

"Then would you like to hear where I am?"

"I guess so."

"You don't sound sure."

"I'm not. I don't know how much more I can face right now, and knowing how much you do or don't love me won't make things any easier."

I pushed myself away from the table and stood up. Out back, I could see Daisy using her nose to roll her ball around the yard. A dog's life? Tell me about it.

"When you are sure, let me know."

She nodded but didn't say anything. She was already crying by then anyway.

What I had wanted to tell her was that I had never loved anyone as well as her, *could* never love anyone as well, that she was everything for me to love. I had even thought about our wedding day, how we might move to Grandmother's farm, she and I, and give Ruth the house in town. Or if Abby didn't mind a housekeeper and Ruth could stand to share a house with another woman, we could all live on the farm and sell the house in town. Was that too much to ask, too much to expect from life? Evidently, it was. But then, nobody was asking me.

Eugene Yuill still wasn't home. Neither had his patrol car gone anywhere in his absence.

With a wave at the white concrete-block building that housed the *Oakalla Reporter,* I cut through the orchard between me and Hal Fortune's beehives and headed south. As I passed between Pete Nelson's house and Milo Thomas's house, I noticed that both stood under Pete's carport staring at me. Apparently they had just come from the post office because each held an *Oakalla Reporter* in his hand. The way they were looking at me, intent, it seemed, on my every step, I had to wonder what I had done wrong? Nineteen sixty-two. That was probably it. They had looked for "Doc Remembers" and discovered it wasn't there.

Rupert Roberts was in his backyard, rototilling his garden. I watched as tomato vines, squash vines, goldenrod, and cornstalks were all turned under the soil. To me, gardening was like cooking, something that I enjoyed when somebody else did it, but ever since his retirement, Rupert had taken to it like the proverbial duck to water. It seemed that every time I went in search of him, I found him here.

Seeing that he had only a couple more swaths to make, I sat down on his overturned wheelbarrow and made myself comfortable. Rupert and his wife, Elvira, lived in a small white bungalow at the intersection of south Berry Street and Madison Road. With a lot more yard than house, Rupert had converted part of it into the garden that seemed to grow every year, just as Ruth's and mine shrank. I admired his serenity, his ability to fill his life with all of those small moments that he had missed while he was working. The day I retired, they would probably carry me feet first out of my office.

Rupert shut off the rototiller and started my way. I scooted over to make room for him on the wheelbarrow. The sun, which had been fighting clouds all morning, finally broke through and blessed us with its warmth. Even at that, the wind was still cold.

"Morning, Garth. What brings you here?"

A tall, thin, somber man with large workingman hands and bloodhound eyes, Rupert Roberts was the only three-term sheriff in the history of Adams County and one of the few people that I would trust with my life. Ours hadn't always been a placid friendship, but it had always been a sure one. And it was he, while sharing a fifth of Wild Turkey and his thoughts on life, who had given me the tarnished special deputy badge that I now carried in my wallet.

"I ran out of any place else to go," I said.

"That bad, huh?"

"Yeah. You could say so."

Rupert pulled a handkerchief from his back pocket to wipe some sweat from his brow. "You here to tell me about it or involve me somehow?"

"Involve you. If I can."

Rupert put away his handkerchief and took out the tobacco pouch that Elvira had given him the same Christmas that I had given Ruth her moccasins. My gift to him that year was a package of chewing tobacco. He gave me a gold nugget. Aeons ago, it seemed. "Involve me in what?" he asked, once he had his chew of tobacco in his mouth.

"You know Doc Airhart died?"

He nodded then spat at a grasshopper that had crash-landed at the edge of the garden. Righting itself, the grasshopper took off for safer ground.

"I also know his memoirs weren't in your paper this morning. Is there a reason for that?"

"I can't find them. I have reason to believe that Aunt Emma either has them or knows where they are, but if she does, she's not admitting it."

"Do you want me to help you look for them?"

His offer surprised me. Since his retirement, Rupert had stayed as far away from law enforcement as possible. And now that his garden was through for the year, he and Elvira soon would be heading for their winter home in San Angelo, Texas.

"Not at the moment. I want you to help me look for Eugene Yuill," I said.

"He's missing?"

"Since yesterday afternoon. Maybe even before that."

"Then who's been patrolling the streets?"

"Nobody."

That bothered him more than he wanted me to know. He spat in disgust. "Somebody has to be out there, Garth. If he only looks like he's on the job."

"I know that. Who do you think's been plugging the dike ever since you retired. We had it all, Rupert, when you were sheriff and Clarkie was deputy. It hurts to think what we've had since then."

"For me, it's been a whole lot of peace, Garth. A whole lot of time on my hands I never had before."

"Not on mine."

"That's not my fault. I paid my dues, just like you're paying yours."

"So why did you offer to help now?"

"I offered to help you find Doc's memoirs. Nothing

more, Garth. And that's only because Elvira will give me no peace unless I do."

The sun went under a cloud, and the day was suddenly cold. I rose and tried to get my blood going again.

"Thanks for nothing," I said. "I can probably find those myself."

"So you don't want my help?" It seemed all the same to him.

"I didn't say that, damn it. Sure, I want your help. If only to get you off your duff again."

Rupert rose, spat one more time before heading back to his garden. "I'll see what I can do, then."

"Nineteen sixty-two," I said. "What do you remember about it?"

"Not much. I was stationed up at Rice Lake then."

A former army MP and then a Wisconsin state trooper, Rupert had waited until his fifties to run for sheriff.

"Then you don't know anything about the body they found near Wildwood Bridge?"

"Heard about it, that's all. Why don't you ask Ruth?"

"Intended to this morning, but I forgot."

"Other things on your mind?" For all of his seeming disinterest, Rupert was at times too perceptive.

"Yeah," I said, not wanting to talk about it. "Other things on my mind."

"I suppose Doc's death did change a lot of things."

"Yeah, I'm certain it did. See you around."

"Garth?" he said before I could leave. "Why the interest in the body at Wildwood Bridge?"

"Nineteen sixty-two. It's my understanding that's the year they found it. Doc was just about to remember 1962."

He nodded but didn't say anything. A moment later I left.

Pete Nelson and Milo Thomas watched me from the

time I left Rupert until I reached Gas Line Road. I didn't like their eyes in my back or the fact that they hadn't seemed to move since I saw them last. They couldn't be that upset about Doc's missing memoirs, or could they?

I returned to Eugene Yuill's house where after five minutes of banging on his door and shouting myself hoarse, I decided to take matters into my own hands. Never had it worked before, so I wasn't surprised when my gold Visa card failed to trip the lock on Eugene's front door. I had to crawl in his front window instead.

The first thing that I noticed was how cold it was in there. Eugene's only sources of heat were a small gas stove in the living room and an electric space heater in both the bathroom and his bedroom. All were turned off and had been for some time.

For a bachelor who entertained guests about as often as I roller-skated, Eugene kept his house fairly neat. Though you couldn't bounce a dime off of it, his bed was made with the pillows fluffed and the covers pulled up to them. There weren't more than two days' worth of dishes in his sink or two weeks worth of crud in his toilet. Even his floor had been swept and his furniture dusted within the past year or so. But there was an old bachelor smell to the house—one of stale sweat and mildew—that I couldn't stand for long. Perhaps because in it, I smelled the ghost of Christmas future.

After raising all of Eugene's blinds and opening another window, I began to search his house to see what I could find that might tell me his whereabouts. His body would have been a dead giveaway, but that would have been too easy. I had to settle for the extra set of his car keys that hung on a sixteen-penny nail just inside his back door. I knew that they were his extra set because his regular key ring was a foot in diameter and on it Eugene kept the keys to his house, feed truck (now up at the Marathon for repairs), and the patrol car, along with those for the jail, city building, elevator, and whatever else he had ever needed a key for. Eugene might be slow of foot and sometimes short of heart, but he was never going to find himself locked out in the cold.

I opened the trunk of Eugene's patrol car and saw something that I didn't like. To my untrained eye, it looked like blood. A black pool of it had gathered and hardened there.

Using Eugene's phone, I called Abby at home, but she didn't answer.

Then I called her at the hospital and found out that she was in surgery. I told them to have her call me at home when she got out.

CHAPTER 5

Ruth had her coat and scarf on and was all ready to go grocery shopping when I arrived back home.

"We need to talk," I said.

"Over lunch," she answered, then left.

With nothing else to do, I sat down and waited for Abby's phone call, which came sooner than expected.

"What is it, Garth?" she said, sounding weary.

"I found what I think is some blood in the trunk of Eugene Yuill's patrol car. How soon can you come by here?"

"As soon as I finish my rounds."

"When will that be?"

"Early afternoon sometime. A lot depends on if there are any problems or not."

"You sound bone tired."

"I am, Garth. Of life in general. Why does it always have to be so hard?"

"You're asking the wrong person. I ran out of answers years ago."

"I read your column in the *Reporter.* It was good."

"Thank you."

"And you're a good man, Charlie Brown. Whatever happens, don't you ever forget that."

"For the good it does me," I said as I hung up.

An hour later, Ruth banged in the back door, carrying a sack of groceries in each arm. Without asking, I went out to the garage where her yellow Volkswagen bug was parked, knowing that there would be more sacks to come. Ruth shopped for groceries as if she were feeding a threshing ring, and for the life of me, I never knew where they all went, but go they did. Sometimes I wondered if we had taken in boarders that I didn't know about.

"Is that all?" she asked as I staggered into the house.

"I hope so."

"What's that supposed to mean?" Already she had her scarf and coat off and her favorite iron skillet on the stove.

"Nothing. Forget I said anything." With a lot of shoving and shuffling, I managed to get all of the sacks to fit on the kitchen table.

"Just remember, it doesn't all come out of your pocket."

"Since when?" I asked.

"Since forever. I always buy my own toiletries."

I searched the sacks to see how many "toiletries" I found. Two, if I counted bars of soap. But I knew better than to say anything.

"No meat?" I said when I had finally put away all the groceries and added the sacks to the pile that we kept in the utility room and which we would never use.

"I didn't like the looks of it. I'll tell you one thing, Garth. Howdy Heavin isn't near the grocer his father was. Nearly everything in there has seen its better day." It wasn't her first complaint about Howdy Heavin and probably wouldn't be her last.

"Then what are we having for lunch?" I hoped I sounded as hungry as I felt.

"Cheese sandwiches and tomato soup."

"Better than tuna casserole," I said under my breath.

"What was that?"

"I said it sounds good."

"I bet." She opened a can of Campbell's tomato soup and spooned it into a saucepan. "What was it you wanted to talk to me about?"

"You said over lunch."

"I can wait if you can."

She filled the soup can half full of milk, then filled it the rest of the way with water and began to slowly stir it into the saucepan. The secret of good soup, Ruth claimed, even Campbell's, was to never get in a hurry. At this rate, I might be dead by lunch.

"Okay, what I wanted to talk about was 1962. Specifically the body that Dewey Clinton says he found near Wildwood Bridge."

She momentarily stopped stirring the soup. "That's the first time I heard that. Who told you Dewey Clinton found the body?"

I started to answer then stopped. I'd just remembered something. "*Bodies.* As I now recall, Dewey said he'd found two of them. If I heard him right."

"When did all this come out?"

"Last night up at the Corner Bar and Grill. Dub Bennett and Sniffy Smith were carrying him high about it."

She took a brick of cheese from the refrigerator and

began slicing it. "As well they should. There was only one body, and to my knowledge, Dewey Clinton never found it."

"Who did then?"

"Doc Airhart."

"What would Doc be doing way up there? It wasn't grouse season, was it?"

"He wasn't doing anything way up there. He was county coroner at the time."

"What I mean is, for Doc to be there, somebody had to call him up there. Who did the calling, or did he go there on his own?"

"How should I know?" She started to say, "Go ask Doc," then caught herself. "I don't know, Garth. But it does make sense that somebody probably called Doc up there."

"And Dewey Clinton did live in the area at the time?"

"Yes. There in the bend above Wildwood Bridge. He lived there until he and his folks moved to town a few months later."

"Any particular reason why they moved to town?"

Once she'd sliced the cheese and made the sandwiches, Ruth buttered the skillet, the top side of the sandwiches, and put them in the skillet. Meanwhile I could smell the soup start to simmer.

"Go ask Dewey," she said to shut me up.

"Maybe I will."

"For the good it'll do you."

As it turned out, a grilled cheese sandwich and tomato soup *were* a whole lot better than tuna casserole. For the first time that day, I felt halfway human.

"Good lunch," I said.

"Thank you. You want dessert?"

"What is there?"

"Persimmon pudding. Aunt Emma sent it."

"As a peace offering?" I was hopeful.

"Because she hates the stuff. Someone gave it to her."

"Why not?"

"It's not poisoned, if that's what you're worried about. I already had some."

"I don't suppose there's any whipped cream handy?"

She gave me her what-do-you-want-for-nothing look. "There might be."

"I was hoping."

Ruth set my persimmon pudding in front of me then handed me a bowl of whipped cream. I helped myself then handed the bowl to her.

"Whose body was it that was found?" I asked.

"He wasn't a local man. A professor, I think, from over at Madison. But the grandson or relative of someone from around here. Anyway, he was wading in Pine Creek, fishing, when he slipped, hit his head on a rock, and drowned. At least that's the official version, and I've never heard anything different."

"Who was sheriff then?"

"Maynard Lutes. But he's long since dead."

"And that's all there is to it?"

"As far as I know."

"Then why all of the interest in it?"

"Who says there is?"

"Several people that I can name. Pete Nelson and Milo Thomas among them."

"Why are they so interested?"

"That's what I'm trying to find out. Sniffy Smith says it's because they used to live near where the body was found. Is that right?"

"They did. They had adjoining farms up there northeast of the bridge about a mile or so. But I don't see what that has to do with anything." She plopped a big spoonful of whipped cream on top of her persimmon pudding and began to eat.

"I'm not saying it does. But today when I went to talk to Rupert, I noticed both Pete and Milo had an *Oakalla Reporter.* On my way back from Rupert's, which had to be a half hour later, they were both still standing there where I'd last seen them. Not talking, as I'd expect them to be, but staring at me. As Caesar said about Cassius, 'with a lean and hungry look.'"

"You just lost me, Garth."

"Never mind." By the time I explained it, it wouldn't make sense to me either.

Ruth downed another spoonful of persimmon pudding. "What did you need to talk to Rupert about?"

"I wanted him to help me look for Eugene Yuill."

"What you mean is, you wanted *him* to look for Eugene Yuill while you went about your business."

I wished I could deny it. "He has more time than I do, Ruth."

"That's not the point. He's put in his time."

"Strange that you should say that because that's what he said."

"Then why can't you accept it?"

"Because, damn it, I need his help. Or did. I'm not so sure anymore." I pushed away my half-eaten bowl of pudding. It was good, but I wasn't hungry anymore.

"Go on. I'm listening," she said.

"On my way home from Rupert's, I made a search of Eugene's house. He wasn't there, but I think I found blood in the trunk of his patrol car."

"No chance it's from a dead dog he picked up off the street?" Ruth had suddenly lost interest in her pudding as well.

"There's always that possibility. But no, I don't think

so, Ruth."

"When will you know for sure?"

"As soon as Abby gets here. She's stopping by as soon as she finishes her rounds."

We heard a car pull up in front of the house. Ruth got up to look out the front window. "Speak of the devil," she said.

"She'd be glad to hear you say that."

I ruffled Ruth's feathers a little. But then I meant to.

"Garth, you know I like that girl better than anyone else you've dragged in here. . . When you got that far. So don't be making something out of nothing."

"Sorry, Ruth," I said as I rose from the table. "The way things are headed, I almost wish that you didn't like her. It might make it easier on me."

"Where are things headed?" she asked with her typical bluntness.

"Detroit, it looks like."

Abby waited for me in her dark-red Honda Prelude that had recently turned 100,000 miles but which was still a pure pleasure to drive. It was ironic, but Jessie's mileage was just about that of the Prelude, and she'd never been a pure anything—except pain in the rear.

"Good afternoon," I said as I climbed into the Prelude.

Abby smiled at me. I could feel all of me light up.

"Good afternoon," she said. "Where are we headed?"

"Eugene Yuill's house. That's where his car is."

"You look sad."

"That's because I am."

"Because of Eugene?" Who a few months ago had helped save my life.

"Because of a lot of things. But I don't want to talk about it now."

We drove to Eugene Yuill's house. I was sorry to see that he still hadn't returned home.

"You're right, Garth. It looks like blood," Abby said as she scraped a sample from Eugene's trunk and put it into a small glass jar.

"When will you know for sure?"

"As soon as I get home and run some tests on it. Do you want to come with me? It won't take long."

"I want to, but I need to make an appearance at my office sometime today."

"Then I'll take a rain check. I plan to be home all evening."

"Then I'll be there."

I closed the trunk as we started to leave. "Garth, look at this!" she said as she knelt beside the left rear tire.

I knelt on the ground beside her, placed my hand next to hers.

She said, "You see it, don't you, here on the fender?" She was pointing to a rusty smear of something about four inches wide and six inches long. Whatever it was, it matched what we'd found in the trunk.

"Couldn't it just be rust? Couldn't he have sideswiped a gatepost somewhere? It wouldn't be the first time."

"Then where's the crease the post would have made?"

She went to her car after another jar. Using a scalpel, she collected some of the stain from the fender.

"Satisfied?" I asked when she was done.

"No. I want to look inside the car to see what's there."

I unlocked it for her. "Give me a call when you learn something."

"Don't you want a ride to your office?"

"No. I can walk from here."

"Suit yourself," she said, turning away.

I'd hurt her feelings. It didn't take a keen observer of

human nature to see that.

"I'm sorry, Abby. Blame it on the time of month."

She turned to face me. "I just wish you'd tell me what was wrong."

"It's obvious, isn't it? Everything."

I turned and started walking toward Gas Line Road.

"Are you still coming by tonight?" she yelled after me.

I didn't answer. I was feeling too sorry for myself to care.

CHAPTER 6

I sat looking out my north window, watching the clouds thicken and the day darken. My desk, which was solid oak and my Rock of Gibraltar, and my chair had come from the boiler room of my father's dairy back in Godfrey, Indiana. In winter, I used to love to sit there in the boiler room, which, thick-walled and isolated from the rest of the dairy, seemed the warmest, coziest place in the world. Now, whenever the days grew short and the shadows in me grew long, I always retreated to my office, the same desk and chair, where I would hide until the well filled up again.

The phone rang. It was Abby. "It's blood, type AB positive."

"On the fender, too?"

"Yes."

"What about inside the car?"

"There wasn't any there."

"Shit," I said.

"It gets worse. I called the hospital to check on Eugene's blood type. He's AB positive."

In February, Abby had set Eugene's broken ankle then seen him through a full recovery. Since then, Eugene had been singing Abby's praises to whoever would listen.

"You know what this means, don't you?" I said.

"No. Besides the fact that Eugene might be dead."

"It means that somebody should probably do an autopsy on Doc."

Dead silence on the other end.

"Or don't you agree?" I said.

"I agree. I just can't do it."

"Then have Ben Bryan."

"I'm not sure Ben can do it either. He told me as much."

"Well, surely to God somebody can do it."

"I'll call Ben and see what he says."

"If it weren't for Eugene and Doc's missing memoirs, I wouldn't insist."

"I know that, Garth." More silence then she said, "You never answered my question. Are you coming by later?"

"As soon as I do a couple things here."

"How about I fix us some supper?"

"Best offer I've had all day."

There was a pause before she said, "No, it's not."

I had to smile. "I'll be sure to be there, then."

She laughed, I laughed, we hung up.

I went to the morgue where I began to pull out back issues of *Freedom's Voice,* the forerunner of the *Oakalla Reporter.* I thought, as I piled April 1962–June 1962 on top of the harvest table that had come with the building, that one of these days I had to get these on microfilm before they completely fell apart. But that would take money I didn't have.

I found what I was looking for in the May 18, 1962, issue of *Freedom's Voice,* which in itself gave me pause. On May 18, 1962, I started the summer of my senior year in high school, a summer that turned out to be one of the very best of my life.

According to the May 18 article, Dr. James Garmone, age forty-five, a professor of zoology at the University of Wisconsin in Madison, had drowned in Pine Creek below Wildwood Bridge. Apparently he had lost his balance in the swift current there, fallen, hit his head on a rock, and that was that. Sheriff Maynard Lutes and County Coroner William T. Airhart had investigated the accident, but no mention was made of who had found the body. James Garmone was the nephew of the late Cyrus Garmone, but no survivors of James Garmone were listed.

I reread the article to see if I had missed anything. I hadn't.

Continuing on through the May and June 1962 issues of *Freedom's Voice,* I found no mention of any other drownings or deaths along Pine Creek. I pulled out the July–October issues and read them. The only thing that I discovered was a sense of loss as I went from one of the best summers of my life right into the Cuban missile crisis.

I put everything back where I'd found it, the way my father had taught me, and started up Gas Line Road. Gone completely flat and grey, without even a breeze stirring, the day made even the gaudy maples along the way look drab.

As I had hoped, Dewey Clinton was there outside of Heavin's Market astride his bicycle. An old blue-and-white girl's twenty-six-inch Schwinn, with a basket on the front and a kickstand (for God's sake!), the bicycle was more of an embarrassment to me than Dewey ever was, and I wanted to hide behind a tree every time I saw him pedaling around town on that damn thing. But since Dewey, or no one else in town except for our resident juvenile delinquents seemed to mind, I had learned to grin and bear it, as I had the sight of children leading their parents around by their noses. Though I think that way down deep, it cost me something.

"Evening, Dewey," I said. "Waiting for Howdy to get off work?"

He nodded but didn't say anything.

"Aren't you cold?" He wore only his customary black sweatshirt under bib overalls, and it was near freezing now that night was coming on.

He shook his head and again didn't say anything. Dewey, who had never been at a loss for words in my presence before, appeared to be afraid to speak to me. Or maybe he was angry at me for some reason.

"Dewey, is it true that you used to live there in the bend above Wildwood Bridge?"

Dewey looked down at the ground, his eyes avoiding mine. "Long time ago."

"And did you once find a body under the bridge?"

As he shyly looked up at me, then glanced around to see who else might be watching, I was struck by the purity of his eyes, the absolute beauty of his face. With his black curls, bright blue-black eyes, and mischievous grin, he could melt your heart, and break it, in the same instant.

"Yes," he said quietly. Then he raised two fingers so that only I could see.

"You found two bodies there?"

He nodded then put a finger to his lips for silence.

"When did you find the second body?"

Dewey looked confused. Time was not something that

he kept track of like the rest of us.

"Was it after you found the first one?"

"Yes." Still not sure of himself.

"How long was it, Dewey, between bodies? A couple days? A week?"

He began to rock nervously back and forth on his bicycle. I didn't know if I were the reason or if he had a full bladder. It was hard to tell how long he had been waiting there in the cold for Howdy Heavin to come out of the market.

"I don't know," he finally said.

"Did you tell anyone about it?"

"Pop."

"Your father?"

He nodded.

"Did he tell anyone?"

Dewey began to rock even harder. I was getting antsy just watching him.

"Doc Airhart," Dewey said.

"No one else?"

Dewey shook his head no.

"Did Doc Airhart come out there?"

Again Dewey's gaze fell to the ground. "He came. I watched him from the hill. Until Pop made me come inside."

"Was it a man's body or a woman's body? The second one you found?"

Dewey shook his head. Either he didn't know or wouldn't tell me.

"But it was a man's body, the first one you found? A man wearing. . . Look at me, Dewey." I put both hands on my chest where the waders would have been. "Waders?"

He nodded then looked away, back down to the ground. "I done it, Garth. I done it."

"Did what, Dewey?"

But before I could stop him, he gave a violent rock forward, stood on the top pedal, and took off on his bicycle for home. As he did, Howdy Heavin came to the front door of the market to see what was up. Whatever he saw didn't please him because he didn't stop at the door.

"What the hell is going on, Garth?"

Howdy wore a white butcher's apron over his jeans and a checkered red-on-red flannel shirt. With his red hair, thin red mustache, long red sideburns, and farmer's tan that had started to fade now that fall was upon us, he looked a lot like one of the guys that used to dance on *Hee Haw.* Or was I thinking of Ron Howard and *Happy Days?*

"I don't know what's going on, Howdy," I lied. "I asked Dewey how his hammer was hanging, and the next thing I knew, he took off."

"I wish you people would leave him alone," Howdy said, neither hiding his anger nor his disgust at me. "Dewey has enough problems the way it is."

"We people, as you call us, are the ones who have been taking care of Dewey for the most of his life," I said, with some anger of my own. "The last I heard, you weren't around until lately."

That took some of the steam out of him, as he dismissed it all with a wave of his hand. "I'm sorry, Garth. It's been a long day, and I haven't been up to it."

"Problems in paradise?"

"Just in running the grocery business. It's not quite the same as leading a mission."

"But a whole lot safer."

"I'm not so sure of that," he said, sounding as if he meant it. "Some of these women are out for blood."

I thought about Ruth and smiled. Either he would learn and survive in the business, or he wouldn't. For once, it wasn't my problem.

"Hang in there," I said. "It'll get better."

"Or worse," he said as he went back inside.

For supper, Abby served baked salmon, steamed carrots, buttered baby lima beans, and frozen peach yogurt for dessert. If I ate that healthy every meal, I'd probably live to a 110 instead of the 100 I was counting on.

We ate by candlelight in the dining room on a white linen tablecloth with Daisy asleep at our feet. It was something that, over the years, I could probably get used to.

"You talk to Ben?" I asked Abby as I helped her carry the dirty dishes into the kitchen.

"Yes. He said he'd do the autopsy on Uncle Bill if you'd give the eulogy on Sunday."

"I'm not sure I can," I said.

"Nobody in Oakalla knew him any better."

"That's the problem."

She set her dishes down, put her arms around me, and held on. "You'll do fine," she said.

Tonight Abby wore the same jeans, loafers, and light-blue chamois shirt with which she had started the day. But no red lipstick and no bra under her shirt. And once I had my way about it, no jeans either.

We slowly made our way up the stairs toward her bedroom, one less article of clothing at a time. It was sort of like playing strip poker without having to bother with the cards.

"What will Daisy think?" Abby said, not really caring.

"That it beats the hell out of grouse hunting."

At the top of the stairs she was down to her chamois shirt and I was down to my birthday suit. We didn't get any farther for a while. And when we finally did make it to Abby's bedroom, it was to rest.

"That's a first for me, I think," she said as we lay in

each other's arms.

I didn't say anything. I was listening to her heart beat and thinking of Ross McDonald's blue hammer. Of all of the images from all of the books I had read, it was perhaps the most vivid, the most lasting. The blue hammer—the blue-veined pulse of your beloved—still beating. Within it was her life, and yours.

"Garth, are you still with me?"

She raised up on one elbow to look at me. I had seen prettier women, but none any more beautiful.

"Still with you. First in what way?" I said.

"That's my secret," she said, suddenly coy.

"A first for me, too."

"How so?" She was less coy now that the shoe was on the other foot.

I winked at her. "My secret."

She jerked the pillow out from under me and hit me with it. "Cad," she said.

I wrestled with her and won. "Ready for round two?" I said.

"So soon?" she said, exploring the possibilities.

I just smiled.

I left shortly after midnight. I didn't want to leave, and Abby didn't want me to leave, but I knew that if I stayed, it would be a whole lot harder to leave in the morning. Besides, I was one of those odd birds who liked sleeping in his own bed, no matter how short the night. My mornings always seemed to go better if I started them at home.

The night was cold, a winter night by the feel of it. No stars shone in the sky, and nearly every house was dark and still. Twice, I stopped to look behind me. I couldn't shake the feeling that something evil was loose in Oakalla, perhaps at that very moment stalking me. Ruthless and impersonal, it seemed to exist for its own sake, to have no other reason to be, but being itself. Its single-minded purpose frightened me as nothing else had. For in its case, feelings, even if it had any, would never get in the way of expediency. Or to put it more simply, the end would always justify the means.

CHAPTER 7

The next morning I was up and gone before Ruth ever made it downstairs. She had come home from bowling a few minutes after I had come home from Abby's, and at that late hour, I didn't even try to talk to her, which would have been a waste of breath anyway. I could always tell how Ruth's bowling had gone by the way she came in the back door. When the door slammed and the house shook, I knew better than to ask.

The day was no warmer than the night had been, and when I saw my first snowflake of the season, I took that as a sign of things to come.

At the Corner Bar and Grill, I ordered two eggs over easy, hash browns, whole wheat toast, orange juice, and coffee and was surprised to have Hiram working the counter.

"Bernice gone today?" I asked Hiram, referring to the

owner, Bernice Phillips.

"Had to take her sister up to the Rapids to the eye doctor," he said as he worked his way down the counter. "So I'm pulling double duty."

"You haven't by any chance seen Eugene Yuill around, have you?"

"No. But I hear he's missing."

"When was the last time you saw him?" I said.

Hiram thought a moment and said, "Wednesday, about midnight. He stopped in for a Coke, said he was headed for the south end of town before calling it a day."

"He say why he was headed for the south end?"

He shrugged as he poured Kenny Cleaver a cup of coffee. "Routine patrol, I think. He'd been everywhere else in town that night."

"Who was in here then?" I said.

"The regular euchre crowd. Sniffy Smith, Dub Bennett, Pete Nelson, Milo Thomas, one or two others."

"Was Dewey Clinton in here then?"

"No. He and Howdy Heavin had left about an hour earlier."

"When did the others leave?"

"About the time Eugene did. That's when the game broke up anyway. I shut her down shortly after that."

"Thanks, Hiram. You've given me a starting place."

On the pretense of refilling my coffee cup, Hiram drew close so that no one else could hear. "What are your chances of finding Eugene alive?" he said.

"Off the record, Hiram, not good. Not good at all."

"He was trying to do a good job. I'll say that much for him."

I nodded in agreement and tried not to think about it.

A few minutes later, I left the Corner Bar and Grill and headed for the south end of town where I went door to door asking about Eugene Yuill. No one that I talked to, however, remembered seeing him Wednesday night, until I got to Myrtle Baker's house. Myrtle didn't remember seeing him either, but she had called him earlier about Dewey Clinton's cats. One of them, it appeared, was in heat and the "damndest cat fights you ever saw were breaking out all over the place." In Myrtle's words, not mine.

Myrtle Baker was a spry seventy-two-year-old widow, who had been married to a trucker, Ivan Baker, at sixteen, and who had a pet spider monkey named Clarence who, had he been registered, could have voted in the last election. And while she didn't object to Dewey's cats "getting their wick trimmed once in a while," she and Clarence did need their sleep. I told her I understood.

Myrtle Baker and Dewey Clinton were neighbors and had been for years. She lived in the second house north of the railroad on Fickle Road. Dewey lived in the first house north of the railroad. Hers was a neat two-story white frame house with narrow siding, a steep roof, and a straight-as-an-arrow red brick chimney that ran all the way to and beyond the south gable from the ground up. Dewey's was a small grey frame house badly in need of paint. Its yard, which never grew good grass even in the best of times, was now mercifully buried in leaves, as were his gutters and eaves. Dewey's bicycle, along with his lawn mower, rake, and snow shovel, stood on the concrete slab that served as Dewey's front porch. So I knew that he was home. Whether he would answer the door might prove another matter.

"Dewey, you in there?" I asked, after knocking and receiving no answer.

"No," I swore I heard him say.

I stepped back off the porch to look at the brown brick chimney that still wore the black creosote scars from last year's flue fire. Unless my eyes deceived me, that was smoke coming out of it.

"Come on, Dewey, I know you're in there."

"No, I'm not."

I opened the front door, which I should have done in the first place. I don't know who was more surprised, Dewey, or I, or the twenty or so cats that went diving for cover. Stepping back outside, I took a deep breath of the outside air.

"Dewey, you need to change your litter boxes more often."

"That's what Howdy says."

"Well, Howdy's right. Why didn't you answer the door?" Dewey, barefooted, had come out on the porch with me.

"Didn't know who it was," he said, looking down at his toes.

"Aren't your feet cold?"

He wiggled his toes, smiling as he did. "No. Not yet."

"Then I won't keep you out here long."

He shrugged as if to say it didn't matter to him.

"What I need to know, Dewey, is whether Deputy Yuill came by here last Wednesday night?"

Dewey kept his eyes on his feet. "Don't know."

"Dewey, look at me."

"Can't."

"Why not?"

"I'm a bad person. I do bad things."

"Such as what, Dewey?"

"Kill people."

"Who have you killed lately?"

"No one."

"That's what I thought."

Dewey raised up on one foot and then the other, as if

the cold concrete was finally getting to him.

"So you didn't see Deputy Yuill Wednesday night?"

Dewey began counting backwards on his fingers. "No. . . Yes. . ."

"Which is it, Dewey?"

"He was here. I didn't see him."

"You stayed inside?"

He nodded. "Trouble with the cats. He was mad at me."

"Did he yell at you?"

Though it was an effort, Dewey raised his head to look at me. "He said if I didn't do a better job keeping them home at night, he might have to shoot some of them." Dewey's eyes had come alive. So had his voice. "I told him he couldn't do that. They are *my* cats!"

"I thought you said you didn't talk to him."

"Didn't," he said defiantly then went inside and closed the door.

Two blocks later, on my way back up Fickle Road, I met Howdy Heavin who was leaving by his front door on his way to work. Today he appeared more on top of things than he had last evening. His confidence was back, along with his smile. He seemed almost eager to get to work.

"Morning, Howdy," I said. "You're looking chipper today in spite of the weather."

"I'm feeling chipper today. There's nothing like a good night's sleep to put the starch back in your spine."

I yawned, wished I could say the same. "You didn't by any chance see Deputy Yuill in the neighborhood late last Wednesday night, did you?"

"How late?" he asked.

"Sometime after midnight."

He shook his head. "No. I was in bed by then. You might ask the folks, though. They're the night owls around here."

"They inside?"

"Eating breakfast, I think. If they haven't finished by now." He saluted me and cheerfully headed off to work.

Howard and Elizabeth Heavin had run Heavin's Market there in Oakalla for as long as I could remember. Though in some ways an odd couple—Howard tall, taciturn, and thin, and the brains of the operation; Elizabeth short, gregarious, and stout, the heart and soul—they both had good business sense, and they both had the sense to know when to lead and when to follow. Also, at least against the outside world, they presented a united front, even when one, or both, were wrong.

Howard, reluctantly it seemed, let me in their back door and invited me to sit at their breakfast table. I felt vaguely uneasy, like an unwanted guest, though I didn't understand what I had done wrong. It wasn't until I sat down and had been served a cup of coffee that I began to see what was going on.

Busy with their business all of their married lives, Howard and Elizabeth were now in each other's way, and likely at each other's throat. Though a large airy kitchen, wood paneled and brightly decorated with Elizabeth's collection of teapots, it seemed small and close with both of them in there.

"So," Howard said, trying to find something to do with his hands, "what brings you to our side of town?"

"You heard that Eugene Yuill is missing?" I said.

Howard and Elizabeth exchanged glances. "We heard," he said.

"Well, at last report, he was in the south end of town sometime after midnight Wednesday night. I just wondered if by any chance either of you had seen him?"

Again Howard looked at Elizabeth. Again she looked at him. Neither one seemed to want to do the talking.

"What time was that again?" Howard said.

"Sometime after midnight is all I know."

"I was in bed by then. How about you, Mother?"

"I told you not to call me that," she snapped. "I'm not your mother."

Howard looked deflated, as if all of the life had just gone out of him. "But I've always called you that," he protested.

I set my coffee aside and rose from the table. "Maybe I'll come back another time," I said.

Angry, Howard said, "Now see what you've done. You've run Garth off."

"That's nothing compared to what you've done," Elizabeth fired back at him. "Here we sit. . ." She seemed to search for the right word. "Strangers in our own home."

"Elizabeth," Howard warned. Then he said to me, "She's mad at me because she doesn't have enough to do anymore. I keep telling her she needs to find a hobby. We both do, for that matter."

"I have a hobby. I collect teapots," she said. "You're the one that needs the hobby."

"I just got through saying I did."

"Why don't you both go back to work?" I suggested. "Part-time anyway. I hear Howdy could use the help."

The look that Elizabeth gave Howard would have killed a weaker man. "I told you that would happen, Howard Heavin. I told you."

"Now, Elizabeth. . ."

"Don't you now Elizabeth me. Howdy's not up to the job. You and I both know that."

"Well, he ain't going to learn with us breathing over his shoulder. Or picking up the pieces every time things fall apart. We tried it that way before. Remember? It wasn't until the army he got himself straightened out."

"Air force," Elizabeth said, suddenly weary. "It wasn't

until the air force. At least get your facts straight."

Howard threw up his hands in disgust and stalked out of the room. I sat back down again because it seemed Elizabeth needed the company.

"How long has it been like this?" I said.

"Ever since Howdy came back. We're not the same people anymore."

"It really might help if one or both of you did go back to work."

She shook her head, looking defeated. "No. Howard wouldn't hear of it. Howdy either. He likes to do things his own way."

"It's probably his military background."

"No. He's always been like that. Headstrong, I believe is the word for it. But I guess he gets it honestly."

"Are you going to be all right?" I asked.

"Have to be," she said. "Only the strong survive."

It wasn't until I was outside again that I realized that she hadn't told me whether she'd seen Eugene Yuill or not.

Abby was just backing out of her drive on her way to the hospital when I walked by. She stopped when she saw me. I went over to her.

"Good morning," she said after rolling down her window. "Is that snow I see on my windshield?"

"It appears to be. How are you this morning?"

"A whole lot better than I was at this time yesterday morning. How about you?"

"I'm doing okay, I think. I'd be doing a lot better if I could find Eugene Yuill."

"No luck so far?"

"Not so far. He was in the south end of town after midnight on Wednesday. That's all I know."

"Do you think you should ask for help?"

"I have. Rupert turned me down."

"I mean the state police."

Abby was right. There *was* snow collecting on her windshield. I scraped some off and made a pea-sized ball out of it that I flipped out into the street.

I said, "Why don't we wait until after Doc's autopsy? Eugene could just as easily have stopped a speeder who took offense, as been somewhere that he shouldn't have. If so, the state police won't be much help."

"And you say Ruth's stubborn."

"I just don't like involving outsiders unless I have to. The best they usually do is muddy the waters."

"But you do think you'll find him?"

"Eventually."

"At no danger to yourself?"

"I didn't say that."

"I can't bury you and Uncle Bill in the same week."

"You won't have to," I promised, then bent down and kissed her good-bye.

I spent the rest of that Saturday looking for Eugene Yuill. I didn't find him. When I at last returned home, it was cold, dark, and snowing—big fat flakes that filled the air but melted almost as fast as they hit.

Ruth had left a note on the kitchen table saying that she had gone to play euchre with the "girls," so I fixed me a tall bourbon and ginger ale, popped me a bowl of popcorn, and sat down to watch what in any other year would have been the baseball play-offs, but tonight was a documentary on baseball. Like a lot of things that I used to love, both baseball and television had lost favor with me over the years. Part of the problem was with them, part with me. But intertwined as they were with the fabric of it, I couldn't imagine my life without them.

So I drank my bourbon, ate my popcorn, and fell asleep on the couch.

CHAPTER 8

It snowed on and off throughout the night, ending right about the time that I was getting up. As I looked out the kitchen window, it was strange to see snow on the ground with the trees still dressed in their fall colors, stranger still to see it piled atop Ruth's roses. Just a couple years ago, there had been a hard freeze in June, and looking out at our frosty yard amid the bright green leaves of near summer, I had thought that the world had turned upside down. But today the paradox troubled me even more. Snow on the roses. What next?

"Something bothering you, Garth?" Ruth asked, as she brushed by me to put the coffee on.

"There's snow on your roses."

"So?" She didn't even bother to look. "They're about done for anyway."

"It just looks strange, that's all. Out of place."

I sat down at the kitchen table. Ruth went on about her business. Discussing metaphysics with Ruth was like trying to talk religion with Doc Airhart. They tried it once, didn't like it, and that was that.

"I'll tell you what's strange," she said as she fired up the stove. "It's seeing you asleep on the couch with the television on. I thought you'd be keeping Abby company."

"I was supposed to be writing Doc's eulogy."

"Is that today?"

"Two o'clock at Fair Haven Church. Visitation starts at one. Abby and I will be leaving shortly after noon if you want to go with us."

"No. If it's all the same to you, I think I'll drive. That way I can come and go as I want."

"It's all the same to me. But after breakfast, I'm going to be scarce. I owe Doc at least that."

Ruth took a pound of bacon out of the refrigerator and about a half-dozen eggs. The menu, which appeared to be bacon and scrambled eggs, suited me just fine.

"I take it you haven't found Eugene Yuill yet?" she said.

"Not yet." I told her what I had found out.

"So do you think Dewey Clinton's involved in some way?"

"I don't see how, Ruth. Despite what he says."

"Stranger things have happened, Garth. You of all people should know that."

She put the bacon on to fry. If there was a better frosty-morning smell than coffee and bacon, I had something to look forward to.

"I still don't think he's involved, Ruth. He's not smart enough for one thing."

"How smart do you have to be to hit someone over

the head and dump him in the trunk of his car?"

"You have to be smart enough to be able to drive his car afterwards."

"You might have a point," she agreed.

It was a small victory, but I'd take it. With Ruth, I didn't have many.

"Any other thoughts on the subject?" she said.

"None that I can make any sense out of."

"Well, I've been doing some asking around and have some news for you, if you're interested." she said.

"Asking about what?"

"Pete Nelson and Milo Thomas, among other things."

"I'm interested," I said.

She cracked the eggs into a mixing bowl, added salt, pepper, paprika, and milk, and began to beat them with a whisk. "I already told you that Pete Nelson and Milo Thomas once owned adjoining farms there in Monroe Township."

"Which is where again?"

She gave me a menacing look. She hated to be thrown off stride when she was gathering a full head of steam. "There to the northeast of Wildwood Bridge. I'd say within a mile."

"What's there now?"

"Not much except the land itself. They sold the farms and abandoned the buildings when they moved to town. Anyway," she said, anxious to get on with it, "it's not important where the two farms were, but who owned the land there on the bluffs of Pine Creek behind them."

"Who was?"

"James Garmone."

"Who is?" Because I'd forgotten.

"The professor who drowned under Wildwood Bridge."

"Tell me more," I said.

"There's not much more to tell. According to my sources, James Garmone willed the land to the University of Wisconsin, and they've owned it ever since."

"How many acres are there?" I said.

"Eighty, I believe."

"Hardly enough to kill a man for. Unless there's oil on them?" I figured it was worth a shot.

"You know better, Garth. No gold either. I checked."

"So we're at a dead end?"

"Unless you can make something out of this. Right about that time, Pete Nelson and Milo Thomas went together and bought an expensive Holstein bull. It was the making of both of their dairy herds."

"Are your sources saying that the money had to come from somewhere else?"

"That's what I'm saying. I know for a fact that they were both poor as church mice up until then."

"And they've done well since?"

Ruth took time out to turn the bacon. "You figure it out, Garth. Once they sold their farms and moved to town, they haven't turned a tap since."

And they both had nice houses. And if I was to believe the *Oakalla Reporter*, their wives spent a lot of time traveling, some of it abroad. So I'd say they had done very well.

"What made them decide to sell out and move to town?" I said.

"The government." I could almost hear her teeth grind at the mere mention of the word.

"How so?"

"You remember when they paid all of those dairy farmers to slaughter their herds a few years back? Pete Nelson and Milo Thomas were the first ones in line."

"So you might say they're opportunists."

"You might say that." She began to take up the bacon.

"But I had another word in mind."

At twelve-fifteen, Abby and I left in her Prelude for Fair Haven Church. She wore a plain black dress that went well with her rosy red cheeks and yellow hair. I wore the grey suit (along with the blue shirt and red tie) that I usually wore to church at Christmas and Easter and which was the only suit I owned. The clouds had started to part, and some sky had started to show through. Nearly gone now, the snow lay in puddles along the street, which, come morning, would no doubt wear a glaze of ice. Monday, that would be. The first day of the so-called workweek.

"How are you holding up?" Abby asked. Once she arrived at my house, she had switched seats to let me drive.

"Not too bad. How about you?"

"Okay, I guess. I just don't have much enthusiasm for anything, including my work, which I normally love."

"You seemed pretty enthusiastic the other night."

She blushed as she remembered. "I guess I'm not dead yet."

I smiled as I remembered. "Not by a long shot, I'd say."

"But you know what I mean?"

"Yeah, I know what you mean."

"Do you think we'll ever get it back, our joy I mean?"

I watched the purple (my favorite), orange, and yellow trees whiz by as we sped north on Fair Haven Road. "I can almost guarantee it."

"From someone who's been there?"

"From someone who was asking himself that same question before you came along."

"And now that I'm thinking about leaving you?"

"I'll cross that bridge when I come to it."

"I couldn't stand not being the joy of your life."

"You won't have to," I promised.

Fair Haven was a beautiful brick country church, the

one I always pictured in my mind when I heard the song, "Church in the Wildwood." Situated among hills, dales, and forest, it'd always had a quietness, a peace about it that I found in no other church. Grandmother Ryland first introduced me to it when I was five, and we attended there on and off, whenever there was a special service or we were running too late to make the Methodist Church in town.

First a Lutheran Church, now nondenominational, Fair Haven had a small brightly lit sanctuary that seemed to admit light no matter how dreary the day or how low the sun in the sky. Grandmother said it was the glow of the Holy Spirit, burning with its own divine fire. And I had a hard time doubting her—even during those days when God and I were working opposite sides of the street.

"We're here," I said, as I got out and held the door open for Abby.

"So we are."

"Have you heard from Ben Bryan yet?"

"No. Have you?"

"Soon, I'm thinking."

Fair Haven couldn't hold all the people who turned out for Doc's funeral, not even after we put folding chairs along the back and in the aisles. Flowers filled the small chancel and spilled out over the altar until you could barely see Doc's casket. As I made my way to the pulpit, I caught one last glimpse of Doc before they closed the lid on him for good. He looked smaller than I remembered him, and thinner, not at all like the giant of a man that I was about to eulogize.

What I tried to say was that even though he professed no religion, and in fact had not set foot inside a church since World War II, Doc was a holy man. Medicine was his religion, as healing was his trade, and all of us in Oakalla owed a huge debt to him for practicing it so well. As for eternity, or the promise thereof, I didn't know, didn't want to speak for God, didn't think it mattered to Doc.

Look around you, I said, you'll see his legacy everywhere—in yourselves, your children, their children. What is immortality but the ongoing of life, and Doc's spirit would live on in us as surely as it had up until now. Caring, compassion, love of the good, and dedication to the truth, those were all part of Doc's legacy. But his greatest legacy was Doc himself, his steadfast witness, his day-in-and-day-out testimony to the beauty and glory of life—when it is lived true and truly lived, when it is done right. And while I was proud to call him many things—healer, thinker, poet, and citizen—I was proudest of all to call him *friend.*

When I finished, Abby was waiting with a smile as I returned to my seat. "You did good," she whispered, as she put her arms around me. Then we both broke down.

Rupert Roberts, Ben Bryan, and I were among Doc's pallbearers. After Doc's graveside service and while Abby was picking a rose from atop his casket, I went to where Rupert and Ben were standing.

"Afternoon, gentlemen," I said. "You both clean up pretty well."

It was one of the few times that I had seen either one of them in a suit. Once he'd retired as sheriff, Rupert was loathe to wear anything that even resembled a uniform. After forty years as a mortician, Ben Bryan felt the same way.

"You don't clean up so bad yourself," Ben said.

We looked out over Fair Haven where the rolling rows of tombstones stood among the pines and cedars.

"You have the results of Doc's autopsy?" I asked Ben.

He coughed, looking to Rupert for help.

"I take it that's a yes."

"Doc was murdered, Garth," Rupert said. "At least

that's what Ben believes and so do I."

Even though it was the verdict that I was expecting, it still came as a shock. "Doc didn't die of a heart attack. Someone smothered him," Ben said.

"But Doc was smiling when we found him," I said.

"Maybe he was expecting it. Maybe even hoping for it."

I looked at Ben for an explanation.

"Doc's health was failing, Garth. You and I both know that. He had maybe a year or two more at the most, and towards the end, who knew how those years would go?"

"So you think he set himself up to be killed?" I said.

"Rupert and I were just talking about that. We think that he thought his murder might be a possibility. If it didn't come to pass, well then nothing would be lost."

"Sounds like Doc," I said. "He surely waited long enough before he ever agreed to let me publish his memoirs in the first place." I turned toward Rupert. "Is that what you're thinking, too?"

"Yes."

"Speaking of which, have you had any luck finding them?"

"No. But I'm working on it. What about Eugene Yuill? You had any luck finding him?"

"No. But I'm working on it."

"Then maybe we'll meet in the middle." With a tip of his imaginary hat, he left, as Ben Bryan followed.

"What was that all about?" Abby asked when I rejoined her.

"Doc was murdered. That's what Ben and Rupert think. Someone apparently smothered him as he slept."

"No, Garth!" Abby said in protest. "That means. . ."

"That means I'm glad you don't walk in your sleep. Or you'd be dead, too."

"You don't know that."

"I know that. As surely as we're standing here. So don't think you could have done anything to stop it."

We started walking toward her Prelude. We were the last ones left in the cemetery.

"But *why?*" she said, outraged at the thought.

"I don't know. But do you feel like taking a drive?"

"If that will help me find Uncle Bill's killer."

"It might."

"Then let's do it."

CHAPTER 9

When we left Fair Haven Church, I turned north on Fair Haven Road, then east when we got to Haggerty Lane. At the end of Haggerty Lane, I turned back north again on Road 600 East until I came to the fourth road on our right which was 1250 North and which (I hoped) was the road that would eventually lead to Pine Creek and Wildwood Bridge.

"I just washed the car last night," Abby said matter-of-factly as we splashed through a large mud puddle.

"Be glad it's not summer. Or the dust would be thick enough to bale."

The remains of Dewey Clinton's old house stood a few feet off the road in the last curve above Wildwood Bridge. The house had collapsed in upon itself so that its roof now rested upon its foundation. A green roof by the looks of it, though it was really hard to tell.

"Sad, isn't it?" Abby said as we surveyed the scene.

"Maybe more than we know."

She gave me a questioning look, but I wasn't yet ready to speculate.

Wildwood Bridge was a covered wooden bridge built by J. J. Daniels in 1890. A rusted metal sign nailed to the west end of it instructed horses to cross it at a walk. Inside it, various lovers, schoolkids, vandals, and misanthropes had carved, spray-painted, and burned their messages into its timbers. And I supposed that it was essential to someone somewhere that everyone knew that (1) Donna sucks good, (2)Life sucks, (3)Joe loves Judy, (4) The Class of '97 Rules. But I found it hard to see the poetry in it.

Seeing no one coming from either direction, I parked the Prelude in the middle of Wildwood Bridge, and Abby and I got out to look through its north window at Pine Creek some fifty feet below. Sluggish now that fall was here, and nearly choked with fallen leaves, Pine Creek seeped through a stretch of chutes and riffles before it fell into the deep pool below the bridge and stopped. Or seemed to stop. But when Abby and I crossed over the bridge to look out its south window, we saw that appearances were, in fact, deceiving. Pine Creek hadn't stopped in the pool after all but inched its way through a long limestone glide before it meandered around a bend and disappeared.

"It's hard to imagine someone ever drowning here," Abby said, echoing my own thoughts.

"It is, isn't it? But if we come back next spring, we might change our minds."

I studied the creek awhile longer. Something else about James Garmone's death didn't seem right to me, but I couldn't quite put my finger on it.

"Something bothering you, Garth?"

"Yes. But I don't know what."

We drove on through Wildwood Bridge, up the steep hill on the other side, and around a curve in the road. Traveling almost due north now, we followed the ridge above Pine Creek, which began to flatten out as woods gave way to farmland. But it was strange to see the fields without a house or barn in sight.

"Where have all of the flowers gone?" Abby said.

"You took the words right out of my mouth."

We came to a battered white mailbox that had the name NELSON painted on it in large black letters. Back a long weedy lane was a house, silo, and barn. I pulled into the lane and stopped beside the house.

"You have any other shoes besides those?" I said, looking down at Abby's high heels.

"I might have some tennis shoes in the trunk."

"Then I suggest you put them on."

"What about you?" she said, referring to my suit and wingtips.

I took off my suit coat and tie and laid them in the back seat. "How's that?"

She gave me a smile that raised my blood pressure a little. "Not bad. For starters."

"Are you sure that we really want to do this?" Abby said a few minutes later as she picked a clump of cocklebtrs off of her sleeve.

I bent down to loosen some cockleburs of my own. "Ask me tomorrow."

We stopped briefly for a look inside Pete Nelson's barn, where even the barn swallows had moved out, leaving only the crickets and spiders—one set singing in the sunshine, the other busy laying in their winter's supply of meat. As I glanced at the empty stanchions, the once plaster-tight swallow nests crumbling down upon the whitewashed walls, the spiders and crickets going on about the business of being spiders and crickets, I thought about Robert Frost's poem, "The Need of Being Versed in Country Things" and the line "For them there was nothing really sad" (about man's departure). Though the more often I read that poem, the more I thought I saw a tear in the poet's eye.

"Nothing doing here," I said. We went on.

We stayed in the lane as long as we could, but then at its end had to cross a cornfield that, though bleached white, had yet to be picked. In there among its thick rows, feathers of snow still remained and only added to the isolation that I was starting to feel. Every crackle in the corn, every rabbit and pheasant, every gust of wind only made my apprehension grow. I was relieved when we finally cleared the corn and entered the adjoining woods.

"How much farther?" Abby asked, stopping to pick more cockleburs from her hose.

"God only knows."

"I thought you knew where you were going."

"Up to a point."

But it was easy to tell when we passed from Pete Nelson's woods into James Garmone's woods. For one thing, we had to cross a barbed-wire fence. For another thing, Pete Nelson's woods had been heavily pastured in the past, and it showed. The trees that had survived were mostly thick-trunked sugar maples—all of which had lost most of their tops and were cracked and scarred with age. Multiflora rose had overtaken the gaps between the maples, but it, too, was now dying, perhaps a casualty of the years of assault by the Japanese beetles. Only along the west edge of the woods, where saplings had once again begun to sprout, did it even look like a woods at all.

In contrast, James Garmone's woods, the one that he had willed to the University of Wisconsin, was so thick that Abby and I could barely make our way through it and wouldn't have made our way through it had it been any earlier in the year. Mostly white ash and black walnut, and except for a few gnarled and twisted matriarchs, whose hoary crowns had shaded out everything below, all of its trees were about the same height and nearly identical in size, about a foot to eighteen inches in diameter. In another fifty years or so, as black walnut and white ash become more and more scarce, this woods might be worth a fortune. But I saw nothing that might make someone want to kill for it.

"Watch your step," I said to Abby, who was leading. "The bluffs of Pine Creek are somewhere ahead."

"I'm glad you told me," she said, slowing her pace a little.

When we finally did break out into the clear, what had been a long hard walk seemed worth it. Pine Creek was little more than a silky black thread two hundred feet below us, while on the opposite bluff from where we stood, magnificent century-old pines had buried their roots deep in the limestone crags and now leaned far out over the bluff, as if for a better look. West by southwest, and now low in the sky, the sun dappled the bluffs in light and shadow, and where it fell upon the hardwoods, lit fires—lemon, crimson, and gold.

"I'd say this is worth killing for," Abby said in all seriousness, as she leaned her head on my shoulder.

"For us, maybe. I know I'd kill to keep it."

"But not to have it?"

"No. Beautiful though it is."

We stood on a giant stump that had blackened over time to the color of pitch. It was warm there out of the wind, fragrant with the smell of freshly fallen leaves.

"We'd better go," I said. "We don't want to get caught

out here after dark."

"But it's so peaceful here," she protested. "And so free."

I took her by the hand and led her off the stump. "And so cold once the sun goes down."

Unwilling to go back through the cornfield, which had become a threat to me, I led Abby on a diagonal through the woods toward what I hoped was Milo Thomas's farm. I might as well have saved the extra steps. Milo's farm, right down to his decimated woods, was a carbon copy of Pete Nelson's. They must have gone to the same school of agriculture—Rush Limbaugh U.

"I thought you said this was was going to be easier," Abby said, her dress and my pants now covered with sticktights.

"I thought it would be."

Looking at Milo Thomas's unpicked field of corn, I wished now that we had gone the other way. But with night coming on, we didn't have time to retrace our steps.

"You coming?" Abby said as she took the plunge into the cornfield.

"Coming."

Once inside the field, which was even more tangled with downed corn and jimsonweed than the other, I stopped every few steps to look behind us for whoever might be there. Though it was an irrational fear, grounded in my always-present fear of closed-in places, and the now fast-falling dusk, I still couldn't shake it. Someone *was* out there, keeping a watch on me. Maybe not today, he wasn't. Not here and now in this cornfield, but from somewhere, he was watching, and before this was all over, he would make his presence known.

"How much farther?" Tired of battling the corn, Abby had started to lag behind.

I waited for her to catch up. "Not much farther. I can

see a break up ahead."

"Are you sure we're headed in the right direction? It seems like we've been walking for hours."

"I'm sure."

The reason why I was sure was that it was nearly dark ahead of us, but still light behind. I turned out to be right.

"Thank God," Abby muttered, as she bent down to kiss the ground once we'd cleared the cornfield. "I bet I look like Old Mother Hubbard."

"More like Old Mother Nature," I said as I picked a cornhusk from her hair.

"Thanks for nothing."

We had only gone a few steps when I noticed a path that someone had recently made in the horseweeds. It led into the cornfield a few yards south of where we had come out.

"You see that?" I said to Abby.

"I see that. It looks like this farm has had another visitor lately."

That observation was confirmed when we found where someone had driven up Milo Thomas's lane far enough where he wouldn't be seen from the road and parked there in the weeds.

"I wonder what he was doing here?" Abby said as we came to Road 1250 North and took a right.

"Hard to say. He could even have been a hunter. There are several things in season now."

"Including us?" Apparently Abby hadn't spent all of her time today walking.

"That's a possibility."

"Because of Uncle Bill?"

"He and Eugene Yuill. We find the killer of one, I'm sure we'll find the killer of the other."

"So you're certain that Eugene is dead?"

"I don't see any way around it, Abby. Not after what Ben found out about Doc."

We were nearly to the Prelude when she said, "I want that bastard to pay, Garth. And I don't much care how."

"Ben and Rupert think that Doc might have seen it coming and chose not to get out of the way."

"How so?"

I told her.

"It still doesn't change anything."

"I didn't say it did. I want him as badly as you do but for slightly different reasons."

"Which are?"

"I think he's a real menace to all of us. I think he'll kill again and again, if we don't stop him. Maybe not here, but somewhere. I don't think he can help himself."

"Then you're saying he's killed before now?"

"Yes. That'd be my guess."

"A serial killer? I can't believe that, Garth. Not here in Oakalla."

"Maybe not a serial killer but something else again."

"Which is?"

I shrugged. I didn't have a name for it. But I knew that some people killed to preserve the lie that lay at their heart. "People of the lie" was what M. Scott Peck called them. He also called them evil.

We were on our way back to Oakalla when, as I slowed to take the sharp turn above Wildwood Bridge, I saw the bright yellow willow that seemed out of place amidst the surrounding pines and hardwoods. Stopping the Prelude, I got out to take a closer look at the willow. I thought that I could see a large dwelling of some kind at the edge of the woods behind it.

"What do you see, Garth?" Abby asked from inside the Prelude.

“I don’t know. But it looks like a house.”

“What’s the big deal about that?”

“No big deal,” I said as I rejoined her in the Prelude. “I just don’t remember seeing it on our way in.”

“There’s a flashlight in the glove compartment if you want a closer look.”

I glanced from her to the dwelling, which looked less than inviting there in the twilight. “No. I think I’ll save it for another day.”

As things turned out, it was probably a wise decision.

CHAPTER 10

"I'm famished," Abby said as we pulled into her drive. "But I don't feel like cooking."

"Why don't we call out for Chinese?"

She glared at me. "As hungry as I am, that's not a bit funny."

"Well, when you get to Detroit, you can."

Her eyes softened, became sad. Already I wished I hadn't said anything.

"No hitting below the belt. You promised, remember?" she said.

I didn't remember any such promise but agreed that it was a low blow. "I'm sorry."

"Sorry enough to fix supper?"

"Sorry enough to order us a pizza."

"From where?"

"The Corner Bar and Grill. It's become their Sunday evening special."

"I didn't even know they had a pizza oven."

"Bernice bought one years ago. They've just never used it until now."

"I'm not sure I like the idea," she said.

"And you call me a redneck."

"Provincial, I believe, is the word I use."

"So do you want a pizza or not?"

"A deluxe. Fourteen inch."

I raised my brows in my best Groucho Marx impression. "That would be a deluxe in my neighborhood."

"Forget I said anything," she said with a smile.

While I ordered the pizza, Abby began turning on lights in the house. After the first seven, I thought that she might be having a panic attack, until she came back into the kitchen with an angry look on her face. "Somebody's been in here, Garth. I know he has."

"What makes you think so?"

"I feel it as much as anything. But there are also places where things have been moved and put back again. I can see the dust marks." She was silent for a moment, then said, "Daisy! I don't hear her barking."

"Isn't she outside?" I said, rising out of my chair.

"No. I put her in the basement when I left to pick you up."

I didn't move fast enough as Abby nearly ran over me in her hurry to get to the basement door.

"Daisy? Baby, are you down there?" Abby asked as she turned on the light.

A dog whimper came from somewhere down below.

"Watch yourself, Abby," I said, as she went flying down the steps. But she wasn't listening.

"Over here, Garth," Abby said when I finally got down

there.

Daisy had wedged herself through the smallest of spaces to reach the corner behind the oil furnace. Once in there, she now couldn't get out.

"Shit," I said as I surveyed the scene. "How are we ever going to get her out?"

"Tear out the furnace if we have to," Abby said. "Isn't that right, Daisy?"

Daisy woofed her approval.

"We're not going to tear out the furnace," I said.

"We are if it's the only way to get her out."

"When she gets hungry, she'll come out."

"I'm not willing to wait that long. Are you, Daisy?"

Daisy whined pitifully as if she really had understood the question.

"See?" Abby said.

Feeling outnumbered, I turned on my heels and started for the stairs.

"Where are you going?" Abby said.

"To find her damn ball. The last time I looked, it was outside."

"How will that help?"

"Maybe she'll decide to come out after I bounce it off the wall a few times."

"I'll go get her supper dish."

It took me about thirty seconds to find Daisy's tennis ball, which was right outside the door. It took Abby that long to retrieve Daisy's supper dish from the cabinet under the sink. But that was all the time that Daisy needed to squeeze out from behind the furnace and come racing up the basement stairs with something long and black in her mouth.

Abby took one look at it and headed for the back door. She thought it was a snake.

"What have you got there, girl?" I said to Daisy as I reached down to take what looked like a length of rubber garden hose from her.

But Daisy would have no part of that. She growled and shook the hose from side to side as if it really were a snake and she were intent on killing it.

"Give, *Daisy!*" I said sternly, which was the command that Doc had taught her over and over again.

She dropped the hose on the kitchen floor, but still kept guard over it. I was afraid to reach for it, for fear Daisy would scoop it up again and take off for the basement.

"Do something," I said to Abby.

"Poor baby, I'll bet you're thirsty, aren't you?" she said as she went to fill Daisy's supper dish with water.

Daisy was indeed thirsty. She drank her dish dry, then nudged it across the floor, playing with it as she did her ball. That gave me my chance to pick up the hose and hide it under the sink.

"She's telling me she wants more water," Abby said, when after several false starts, Daisy finally went in the direction of the sink.

"I'll bet she types, too," I said.

"Garth Ryland, you sound jealous."

While Abby's back was turned, I got down on all fours, then limped across the kitchen to paw at her leg. I had forgotten all about the pizza until I heard the front doorbell ring.

"Crap," I said as I scrambled to my feet.

"Serves you right," Abby said, trying her best not to laugh.

When I returned with the pizza, Abby and Daisy were both waiting for me, each with a stern look on her face. "What now?"

"Show him, Daisy."

But in the end, it was Abby who had to show me the ugly welt on Daisy's back where someone had struck her with something—in all likelihood the rubber hose. The long and short of it then was that Abby and Daisy got the lion's share of the pizza, while Garth got Doc's last two Leinenkugel's and called it even.

"Now aren't you sorry you ever doubted her?" Abby said about Daisy, who, stuffed to the gills, was about to fall asleep on her rug.

"She ate half the pizza. How sorry should I be?"

I rinsed out my beer bottles, then after I set them in the sink to drain, folded up the pizza box and jammed it into the waste can. Meanwhile Abby cleared the table and wiped it clean.

"When do you think he came?" Abby said.

"Probably while we were at Doc's funeral. It would be the ideal time, with the whole rest of the town there."

"Then that makes it easy."

"How so?" I said.

"We just look at the list of mourners and see who's not there."

"Sounds easy anyway."

"Then what's the problem?"

"How do we know who's not there?"

"Surely you have some idea by now," she said.

Surely I did, but nothing to hang my hat on. "You ready to start looking?"

"For what?"

"Whatever your intruder was looking for."

"You don't think he found it?"

I walked to the window and back in part to see how well I was tracking. Two beers one right after the other sometimes made that a concern.

"There's only one way to find out," I said.

Abby suddenly looked anxious. “You don’t think he’s still here, do you?”

I nodded in the direction of the window. “No, I think he’s out there. Somewhere.”

“What makes you so sure he’s not still in the house?”

“Because Daisy would have told us so.”

She smiled at me. All was forgiven. “Do you really think she took that hose away from him?”

“It had to come from somewhere.” Though he had more likely lost it behind the furnace while striking at her there.

“We should have bought her a steak instead of a pizza.”

Daisy sighed contentedly in her sleep the way Belle used to as she lay before the fire after a successful hunt. “I think she’s satisfied.”

Abby took the basement because she knew her way around there better than I did. I took the first floor, starting in Doc’s office, which seemed the likely place for the intruder to start. Puzzled, I saw nothing out of place, nothing to indicate that anyone had even been in there since I was last. So if not Doc’s memoirs, what was he looking for?

“Garth!”

Abby’s voice said to come on the run. I did.

“Where are you?” I yelled when I reached the basement steps.

“Doc’s morgue.”

I was afraid she was going to say that.

Doc’s morgue was a deep narrow room that had at one time been a coalbin before Doc converted it to its present usage when he moved here in the 1930s. Furnished with a stainless-steel operating table, stainless-steel cabinets for storing instruments, chemicals, and equipment, a stainless-steel sink, a gas stove for heating water, an inside spigot for washing down the floor, and a huge floor drain, its white walls and ceiling illuminated by bright fluorescent lighting, Doc's morgue (outside of the hospital's operating room and Ruth's bedroom) was probably the most immaculate room in Oakalla. Still I couldn't walk in there without wanting to gag.

It never seemed to bother Doc, though, or Abby either. Each was as much at home there as I was in my office.

"What is it?" I asked from outside the door.

"You'll have to come in to find out."

Abby was sitting at the far end of the morgue with her back to the wall. Standing on the floor beside her was the wooden whiskey keg that had been in there for as long as I could remember. I used to sit on it sometimes when Doc and I would talk. Lying on top of the keg was Doc's claw hammer and several bent nails. Between them and me was the ever-present smell of formaldehyde.

"I take it that you want me to lift the lid on that keg," I said when I finally made it that far.

"If you have the stomach for it."

Abby, the pathologist, was sitting on the floor in shock. I, the uninitiated, had just been asked about my stomach, which had already started to rumble. This didn't bode well for me.

"Just tell me what's in there. I'll take your word for it," I said.

"Bones are what's in there. Or to be more exact, a child's skeleton."

I sat down on the floor beside Abby. After today, I was going to need a new suit. "You have any idea where it came from?" I asked.

"None whatsoever. I'd always wondered why the keg was in here. I know Uncle Bill used to sit on it and talk to me while I worked, or vice versa, but I never could figure out what its function was." She gestured aimlessly, helplessly. "Everything in here has a function, you see. Uncle Bill wouldn't have it any other way." She nodded at the barrel. "Except that."

"So you decided to open it up?"

"Only after I'd shaken it first."

"Well, that seems to solve one thing anyway," I said. "We know what the intruder was looking for."

"Do we? I'm not so sure."

"It stands to reason, Abby. This is not something that very many people knew about. Perhaps only one now that Doc is dead."

"But why would Uncle Bill hide it all of these years?" She was angry at him. "And why didn't he tell me about it?"

"Maybe the right occasion never arose. Maybe he was waiting until after he published his memoirs, or even until after his death."

"And maybe he was protecting someone?"

"That's also a possibility."

"And how could he tell me after his death?"

I smiled at her. "Knowing Doc, he'll find a way."

"So we have a séance, is that it?" She was angry at me now.

"No. We take out those bones and see what they tell us."

"What do you mean *we,* white man?" she said. "I'm the one who has to do the doing."

"And I'm the one who has to take it from there."

She shook her head, looking weary. "Not tonight, Garth. I'm not up to it."

"I'm not either. Let's say we go to bed."

"I want a bath first."

"And I want a shower."

"And I want you to spend the night. After everything that's happened, I don't want to be here alone."

"I planned to anyway."

"Then you'd better call Ruth."

I thought that over and said, "You're probably right."

But I didn't call Ruth.

CHAPTER 11

The next morning I had a decision to make, whether to head home for a change of clothes before I went to work or to go straight to work from Abby's. If I went home, I'd have to explain myself to Ruth, where I'd been and why. Since I wasn't yet up to that, I decided to go straight to work.

"I'll take a look at those bones after a while," Abby said to me at the back door. "I want to check in with the hospital first."

"Call me when you know something. I'll be at work."

"All day?"

"Most of it anyway. I'll have to see after that."

"I love you," she said.

"And I love you."

Daisy followed me as far as the backyard gate where I

took her ball from her and gave it a toss. She chased it down in an instant, but at that I was too quick for her and had the gate closed and locked again before she returned.

Though the morning was cold and there was frost everywhere I looked, the day itself promised to be warm once the sun got its act together. And though it meant high-stepping my way through some weeds, I took the back way to work because I didn't want anyone to see me leaving Abby's house, wearing a day-old beard and yesterday's suit.

I wasn't prepared, however, to find the back door of the *Oakalla Reporter* locked. My printer never bothered to lock it after he left, and I never bothered to see if he had, so it usually stayed unlocked Friday to Monday when I thought of it again. I crawled in a window and made a mental note to ask my printer about it the next time I saw him.

The first thing that I did once I reached my office was to call Ruth to tell her that I was still alive. In a voice as frosty as the day outside, she said that she was glad to hear that and hung up. Abby was right. I should have called last night.

For the next three hours after that, I never got more than an arm's length from my phone as my sources called up to tell me their news, my critics called up to offer me their opinions on my newspaper and to wonder when "Doc Remembers" would next appear, and my fans (both of them) called up to tell me how much they'd liked my column. By the time I finally did get some work done, it was afternoon and I was hungry. Abby's idea of breakfast was a banana and a cup of yogurt topped with wheat germ. That had worn off about midmorning, and then it was a test to see how long I could last without eating my phone book.

At two I finally gave up and went home.

"I won't even ask," Ruth said after taking one look at me.

"Am I that bad?"

"Go look in the bathroom mirror."

I looked in the bathroom mirror. Freddy the Freeloader came to mind.

Back in the kitchen, I said, "I wondered why people kept crossing the street when they saw me coming." I opened the refrigerator and began rummaging through it. "Is there anything to eat in here?"

"Supper's less than four hours away," she said.

"I know that, but I can't last that long."

"Then eat a bologna sandwich. That will tide you over until then."

"I'll eat a peanut-butter-and-jelly sandwich instead."

"Whatever," she said, not caring either way.

"Okay, I'm sorry I didn't call you last night, but I didn't feel up to offering an explanation."

"No explanation would have been necessary. Just a phone call. As I've said more than once, you're an adult. What you do is your business."

"I did mean to call, Ruth."

"Then why didn't you?"

I shrugged. I didn't have anything to offer in my defense. "I will next time. How's that?"

When she didn't answer, I got busy fixing my sandwich. Eventually she'd come around. Unlike me, Ruth didn't hold a grudge for longer than she had to.

"I do have a favor, though," I said as I poured me a glass of milk. "At your convenience, I'd like for you to get a list of mourners from Ben Bryan and see who was conspicuous by his absence from Doc's funeral."

"Any particular reason why?" She had brought up her cooker from the basement and was preparing to can the last of our tomatoes.

"Because someone came into Abby's house and took a rubber hose to Daisy while we were gone."

"How is Daisy?" Ruth asked, stopping her work. She was the one who had helped me find Daisy for Doc.

"She's fine now. But she was a pretty scared pup when we came home last night."

"After being where?"

Between bites of my sandwich, I told her where, then how our night had gone (most of it anyway) once we had arrived back at Abby's.

"I don't see how that list is going to help you any," Ruth said. "Not everybody that was there had a chance to sign it."

"Well, maybe you can fill in the gaps once you get it."

"I haven't said I would yet," she said, her canning temporarily forgotten. "Which brings us to another matter. What do you have to compare it to? What I mean is, if we have no idea who broke into Doc's house or why, then what good will it do us?"

"I have some ideas, Ruth."

"Then I'd like to hear them."

I explained myself as best I could, why I had questions about Pete Nelson, Milo Thomas, Howdy Heavin, and Dewey Clinton. "And there's someone else I'm missing, but I can't think of who it is."

"How so?"

"If I knew how so, I'd know who it was. But something keeps telling me there's someone I'm overlooking."

"So what do you want me to do?" She had returned to her canning.

"First get that list and see who is on it, and then find out all you can about the people I mentioned. Specifically where Pete Nelson and Milo Thomas got the money to buy their prize bull back in 1962? And what Howdy Heavin is doing back here, trying to run a business he obviously has no skill at? And if, in fact, Dewey Clinton did find James

Garmone's body after all?"

"What will you be doing in the meantime?"

"Changing out of this suit, first of all. Then I thought that I might pay Aunt Emma a visit and after that drive out to Wildwood Bridge."

"I thought you were just out there yesterday," Ruth said as she began to load up her cooker with tomatoes.

"I was. But something about the James Garmone's drowning doesn't sit right with me."

"Then I suggest you stop by the *Reporter* and read over the account again before you drive all the way out there in that car of yours."

Ruth no longer bothered to call Jessie by name. Her contempt ran that deep.

"Good idea. But I still want to drive out there to check it out for myself."

She didn't say anything more. She knew that where Jessie was concerned, she would probably get her chance later.

I was almost to the stairs when I remembered what I'd forgotten to ask her. "Ruth, who used to live in that house there above Wildwood Bridge?"

"I already told you. Dewey Clinton and his family."

"No, on the other side. There in the curve east of the bridge."

Ruth's scowl was one of reproach for my not knowing better. "That never was anyone's home, Garth. That was an orphanage.They shut it down about twenty years ago."

"An orphanage?"

"Yes. They call them children's homes now."

"I know what an orphanage is. It just surprises me that there was one there."

Her answer was typically Ruth. "It shouldn't."

After changing clothes, I went out to the garage where

Jessie had been parked for over a week now, which was the one week in the last fifty-two that she hadn't failed me. There were probably others, but they escaped me.

True to form, however, Jessie started on the first try. She always did that when I was expecting the worse and had an alternate plan. Plan B today was to borrow Danny Palmer's wrecker and haul Jessie out to Hidden Quarry and pitch her over a cliff, which was something that I had often threatened to do but so far had lacked the guts.

On my way to Aunt Emma's, I stopped at the *Oakalla Reporter* to get my story about James Garmone straight before I *did* drive all the way to Wildwood Bridge, only to find myself stranded. One look at the morgue told me that someone else besides me had been in there lately. No matter how careful he had been to put things back where he had found them, he had failed in one crucial aspect. Like the currency in my wallet, I always faced the papers the exact same way. Though still in chronological order, some of the papers were inverted, and some were facing down. That small lapse in care surprised me. Anyone who had gone to the trouble of searching the morgue, if he were the same person who had killed Doc and Eugene, should have been smarter than that.

As I read over the account of James Garmone's death, I saw why I had questions about it. Evidently someone else had had questions about it, too, because it was one of the papers that was upside down.

Aunt Emma was outside raking leaves into several piles along Berry Street. She would burn them as soon as the wind was right, which meant that it would blow the smoke into her neighbors' houses instead of hers.

The day had turned out neither as warm nor as blue as I had hoped, and against the chill, Aunt Emma wore a thigh-length dark-green wool sweater with black buttons that looked older than I was. So did her rake, which had a couple of tines missing and whose handle was held together with electrical tape.

"Here," she said, reaching into her sweater pocket and handing me a folded sheet of paper. "It'll save us both time."

"What's this?" I said.

"Read it and find out." She went back to raking leaves.

I unfolded the sheet of paper. Its message, in Doc's handwriting, read: Abby or Garth, whoever gets here first, there was no water in his lungs.

I turned the paper over, hoping that there was more on the other side. There wasn't.

"Is this all?" I asked Aunt Emma, who had stopped to watch me.

"That's all. What do you make of it?"

"What do *you* make of it?" I said. "Surely Doc said something when he gave it to you."

"He did. He said if anything happens to me, give this to Abby or Garth."

"Then why didn't you give it to me the other day when I was here?"

Her wizened old face showed not a hint of remorse. "You weren't looking for it. You were looking for Doc's memoirs."

"Still. . ."

"Still nothing." She reached out for a leaf, dragging the rake perilously close to my toes. "You got what you came for. Now get. I've got work to do."

"Answer me at least a couple questions," I said.

She turned the rake end over end and used it like a cane to lean on. "I'm listening."

"Did Doc say anything to you about what was going on?"

"Only that he thought he might have reason to fear for his life."

"But not why or from whom?"

"No. And believe me, Garth, I'd tell you if I knew." The sadness in her voice said that she was telling the truth. "There aren't many of us old soldiers left anymore, Garth. Not who took their first breath at the beginning of this century."

I tried to imagine what it must be like to have lived that long but couldn't. What I could imagine, however, was the loneliness that came with burying all of your old friends.

"Did Doc indicate to you that his danger might have something to do with what happened in 1962?" I said.

"He let on that that might be the case. Or whatever year it was he was taking on next. We never talked much about his memoirs. Only about the old days."

I noticed that, like Ruth, she didn't say the "good" old days. "You never read his memoirs, then?"

"Didn't need to, Garth. I lived them." Then she handed me her rake and started for the house. "I think I need a drink."

Had I had more time, I would have joined her.

CHAPTER 12

It was downright cold by the time I reached Wildwood Bridge. The sun was headed down, and a chill northwest wind made the shadows seem even nearer.

I drove on up the hill and parked just off the road in what I assumed was the driveway of the former orphanage. Tamarack had taken over the drive and now itself was being overtaken by a tangle of green briers and blackberry bushes. Ahead, the willow that had first caught my eye had since shed most of its leaves, which now lay like yellow feathers in a ring around the tree, as if Big Bird had met his end there. A few yards farther on and right at the edge of what was now woods, vines had claimed the front of the orphanage by attaching themselves to its pillars (six of them in all) and climbing up its face all the way to the roof. I couldn't see beyond that.

Following a path that appeared to have been made by either a car or a truck, I came to two huge concrete lions that sat on either side of the steps, guarding the entrance to the orphanage. They seemed to dare me to try to squeeze by them and go on inside. I didn't take the dare.

Instead, I followed what appeared to be someone's footpath around to the back of the orphanage, where within the shadow of the orphanage itself, it was considerably darker than it was in the front, almost like night. Although I was watching my step, I stumbled in a patch of soft earth and nearly went down. Except the earth shouldn't have been soft there. The ground around it was as hard as stone.

Scraping off the leaves, I saw that a section of ground about three feet wide and six feet long had been recently overturned, but when I dug my hands down into it as far as I could go, I didn't feel anything. A shovel was what I needed. But the last time I looked in Jessie's trunk, there was none there.

Rising, I discovered that I was sweating. Profusely. Already I was soaked to the skin. Then I felt the skin on the back of my neck start to prickle, as if someone were watching me. However, I had seen no one, heard no traffic at all on Road 1250 North.

With the sun almost to the western horizon, I had a decision to make. I could stay here in the near dark and try to dig this out by hand, or I could go for help. Logic said to go for help. So did the feeling in my guts.

Logic also said not to stop at Wildwood Bridge on my way out but to make tracks for Oakalla as fast as Jessie would go. But I hated to waste the opportunity now that I was here, and more, I hated to think of myself as a coward. So after I turned around in the driveway of the orphanage, I slowly headed down toward the bridge, looking for a place to park. I found one at the top of what must have been a lovers' lane years ago before the nettles and jewelweed took over.

After setting Jessie's parking brake, I got out and tried to ease my way down to Pine Creek. The hill was so steep, however, that I began to slide and then had to run just to keep my balance. Right through a patch of nettles and over a sand dune I went, not stopping until I reached Pine Creek. There I knelt at the edge of the creek and tried to wash the sting of nettles away. Sundown, I noted when I rose again. I had planned to be home by now.

I had crossed the creek at a riffle and almost reached the pool below Wildwood Bridge when I heard what sounded like an elephant crashing through the brush down the hill behind me. Then silence, several seconds of it, as I watched and listened for where the elephant might be going from there. Nowhere, it appeared. He had stopped there at the brush at the bottom and the hill and seemed intent on going no farther. Waiting in ambush, perhaps, for me to come back his way.

What had first bothered me about James Garmone's death still bothered me. According to the account in *Freedom's Voice,* he had apparently lost his balance in swift water, hit his head on a rock, and drowned. Even if I disregarded Doc's message to Abby and me, "There was no water in his lungs," and the fact that a dry summer and fall had left Pine Creek a little more than a trickle, I still couldn't find any rocks on which James Garmone could have fallen and hit his head. True, there were plenty of rocks showing on the other, deeper side of the pool, but there was nothing but sand and gravel where I was standing and where James Garmone would have been standing if he were wading and fishing. You didn't wade and fish from deep water to shallow, but from shallow to deep, which was where most of the fish were likely to be.

But thinking that I hadn't given the pool a fair test, and wanting to be absolutely sure, I took off my shoes, socks, and jeans and waded into Pine Creek. If someone came along in the meantime, I'd plead insanity.

The first step nearly took my breath away. The second step left me numb from my knees to my toes. Despite my best intentions, I had no desire to go any further.

I heard what sounded like footfalls and the rattle of something metallic on the bridge above me. Wading in to the bottom of my boxer shorts, I kept trying to feel for rocks with my toes, and at the same time tried to keep an eye on the bridge above me to see what might be going on there. I didn't like the way things were playing out. James Garmone couldn't have fallen and hit his head on a rock, not unless he'd dived from the bridge.

I saw the rock coming an instant before it arrived and instinctively ducked away. Had it been directly on target, however, it would have flattened me.

Kawoosh! It hit the water with the force of an anvil, completely drenching me. For an instant I was too stunned to do anything. Then, in only what can be described as a fit of madness, I took off running—through the water, across the gravel bar, then up the hill behind it.

All for naught, it turned out. When I reached Road 1250 North, he was long gone. The only glimpse that I caught of him was his bicycle, as he rounded the curve there where his house used to sit.

I was on my way to Jessie when I realized that my keys were still in my jeans and that my jeans were still down on the gravel bar. It was then, too, that I first felt the nettles and briers that I had disdained on my way up the hill.

After gingerly making my way down to Pine Creek, I

dressed and started back upstream the way I had first come. There was still plenty of time to catch up to Dewey Clinton before he got to Oakalla. That is, if I could last that long. My legs were a red mass of scratches and welts, and I had bruised my feet on my charge up the hill.

It wasn't an elephant, I soon discovered, that had gone crashing down the hill through the brush. Well, perhaps a white elephant—Jessie. Someone had taken her out of gear, and that was all of the encouragement that she needed to once again leave me high and dry. The irony of it was that, besides the fact that her parking brake was still on, she had escaped with barely a scratch, while I was bleeding from nearly every pore.

Two hundred feet down the side of a near mountain and she had come out with a ding on one fender and a few scratches on her hood. Which only went to prove that there was a God and that I wasn't on His short list. With a sigh, I climbed back up the hill and started toward town, only to be rescued by Ruth in her Volkswagen about an hour later.

CHAPTER 13

"I figured as much," she said as I opened the door and got in. "Maybe now you'll sell that piece of junk."

"Who in Oakalla would buy her? Besides, it's not her fault I'm walking." Limping, to be exact. I could barely put one foot in front of the other when Ruth came along.

"Whose fault is it, then?"

"Mine, for ever trusting her parking brake. And whoever it was that took her out of gear and sent her down the hill."

Ruth turned around in the road and headed back toward town. "Maybe you'd better explain yourself."

I told her how my day had gone after leaving home.

"So you really think it was Dewey Clinton who tried

to drop that rock on you?" She seemed to have her doubts.

"I can't be sure, but I think so. He rode like Dewey anyway. You didn't by any chance see him on your way out of town, did you?"

"I saw someone on a bicycle right after I turned on Fair Haven Road, but I can't be sure it was Dewey."

"Coming into town from the north?"

"He was already in town when I saw him, but yes, he was headed south."

"But you can't be sure it was Dewey?"

"I said not," she snapped. "He had his head down, and it was dark, and I wasn't paying all that much attention anyway."

"It *was* a man, though, and not a woman?"

"If I had to choose one or the other."

We rode in silence for a while. Bright, white, and on the wax, the moon had already crossed the meridian and started down. But only a smattering of stars had so far appeared in what, since sundown, had been a cloudless sky.

"Did you get the list of mourners from Ben Bryan?" I asked.

"I did. Everybody that you named off to me was on it. Except for Dewey Clinton," she said.

"That includes Howdy Heavin, Pete Nelson, and Milo Thomas?" I said, double-checking her.

"If it didn't, I would have told you."

"I'm still missing somebody, Ruth. Or something in me says I am."

"Be that as it may, there's more to it than that. Pete Nelson and Milo Thomas came in a separate car from their wives and went home the same way. Early, Aunt Emma says. Between the funeral and the graveside service."

"Did anybody else leave early that she noticed?"

"Yes. But they weren't on the list."

"Did Abby by any chance call?"

"Not that I know of. Why?"

I felt a twinge of anxiety. She was supposed to call me that morning as soon as she had a chance to study the bones she'd found.

I told Ruth why.

"She probably had something come up at the hospital," Ruth said. "I wouldn't start worrying yet."

"What if you hadn't been worried about me? I'd still be walking."

"That's different. She doesn't drive a pile of junk like you do."

The first thing that we did when we got to Oakalla was to go to Dewey Clinton's house. But Dewey wasn't there. Neither was his bicycle.

From there we went to Heavin's Market, which had closed for the day; then Ruth waited in the Volkswagen while I went inside the Corner Bar and Grill. None of the regulars were there, however, and that included Dewey Clinton.

"Where is everybody?" I asked Hiram.

"I can't figure it, Garth. It's just one of those nights. Maybe they'll all show up later."

"Have you seen Dewey Clinton at all tonight?"

"Nope. Howdy Heavin was just in here a few minutes ago asking the same thing. Why? Is Dewey lost?"

"In a manner of speaking. There are a couple questions I have for him is all."

"Well, if he comes in, I'll be sure to tell him that you're looking for him."

"I'd rather you wouldn't do that, Hiram. Just give me a call at home."

"No luck," I said to Ruth once back in the Volkswagen.

"Where to now?"

"The Marathon. I need to check in with Danny Palmer."

"We seem to be going in circles," Ruth said with some accuracy, since the Marathon service station was east across Fair Haven Road from Heavin's Market.

"It does seem that way."

The Marathon, like the Corner Bar and Grill, was nearly deserted. Only Danny Palmer, the owner, was there.

"Where is everybody?" I asked, wondering if there was some sort of conspiracy that I didn't know about.

"I don't know, Garth." Danny Palmer was Oakalla's Horatio Alger. The oldest of seven children in a family that could barely afford the proverbial pot, he had by hard work, attention to detail, and a zest for life built the Marathon into the best service station around. At the moment, he was working on someone's brakes. "Are you looking for anyone in particular?" he asked.

"Dewey Clinton, if you've seen him around."

"Not since yesterday, I don't think. Why? What's he done now?" Once the brake shoes were in place, Danny began to put the rest of the hub back together.

"I'd rather not say until I'm sure. But I would appreciate it if you'd give me a call if he comes in."

"No problem."

"And I have another favor. Two actually, though I'll only pay you for one of them. Jessie's at the bottom of the hill there east of Wildwood Bridge. I'd appreciate it if you'd tow her out."

Danny laughed. "So you finally made good on your promise after all of this time."

"I wish. But someone else sent her down the hill."

"Ruth?" Danny had the hub back together and was ready to put the tire on.

"No. Not that she wouldn't, if she had the chance."

Danny stood up and used the rag from his back pocket

to wipe the dirt from his hands. "Dewey Clinton? Is that why you're looking for him?"

"What do you know that I don't?"

"Only that when Dewey was in here last evening airing up his tires, he said something about riding out to Wildwood Bridge today. But you know Dewey, how he tends to exaggerate sometimes, so I didn't know if he'd ride all that way or not."

"It appears he did" was all I said.

"You can hardly blame him, if he did roll Jessie down that hill," Danny said in Dewey's defense. "He's heard you talk about it enough."

"Monkey see, monkey do?"

"Something like that."

"You didn't happen to see him today riding by?"

Danny shook his head. "No. I can't say that I did."

"Thanks, Danny." From where I stood, I could see Ruth in the Volkswagen and knew that she was past ready to be home.

"You said you had two favors. What's the second one?"

"At the top of the hill there at the curve east of the bridge is what used to be an orphanage. There's a cleared space behind it where the ground is soft. I thought we might go out there later tonight and dig it up."

Danny shook his head. "No can do, Garth. As soon as I finish up here, I've got a town board meeting." Along with being chief of Oakalla's volunteer fire department, Danny was also president of the town board.

I wasn't all that disappointed. I'd seen enough of that part of the county for one day. Besides, my feet hurt.

"Well, maybe you can take Sniffy and Dub along with you tomorrow morning and have them dig it up."

"For free? Or just which of the two favors are you paying for?"

"Tell them it's their civic duty."

"I'll tell them. But my bet is that it will take more than that to get them out there."

"Such as?"

"Nothing you can name, Garth. Sniffy and Dub aren't very work brickle in their old age, if you hadn't noticed."

"Well if they won't, and you can't find anybody else, maybe I can go myself." Though I hated to take the time away from the *Oakalla Reporter.*

Danny rolled the tire over to the car and set it in place. "I'll see what I can do. But it might be afternoon before I can shake free."

"Then afternoon it will be."

Moments later I followed Ruth in the back door at home. The phone rang the minute we were inside. Since Ruth made no move in that direction, I answered it myself and was relieved to hear that it was Abby calling.

"Where have you been?" she said. "I was starting to worry about you."

"It's a long story. How about if I come over later and tell you about it?"

"That's one of the reasons I called. I don't feel safe here anymore after what happened yesterday. I was wondering if Daisy and I might come over and spend the night with you? I can always sleep on the couch if it's a problem."

"I can sleep on the couch," I said. "But what about Daisy? Our yard isn't fenced."

"She can stay in the basement. And I'll bring her leash for when she needs to go out."

"Ruth will like that," I said in what I thought was a low voice.

"Will it be a problem? Tell me if it will."

"No problem," I said, repeating Danny Palmer's words to me. Which along with "Have a good day" were the watchwords of the nineties. But then again, how original could you be a hundred fifty times a day?

"What will I like?" Ruth asked the instant I was off the phone.

"Taking Daisy out into the backyard for her pooh-pooh," I said, not trying not to smile. "She and Abby will be staying with us for a few days. And I'll be sleeping on the couch," I added before she could protest.

"There's no sense being a hypocrite about it," she said.

"That's not the reason I'm sleeping on the couch. Not the main one anyway. From down here I can better hear what's going on."

Ruth had started to heat up supper, which smelled like ham and beans and corn bread to me. "Are you afraid that someone might have another go at you?"

"I think it's possible, yes."

"And Abby, is she a target, too?"

"Yes. I think we might both be fair game."

"For Dewey Clinton?" She was incredulous.

"That does seem hard to believe."

"Impossible for the Dewey Clinton I know."

"You might be right, Ruth. But it's the Dewey Clinton I don't know that bothers me."

"You can't think he's smarter than he appears, Garth. I've known Dewey all of his life, and I'm telling you, he's not."

"Then why did he try to drop a rock on my head?"

"Maybe he thought he was playing a trick on you." She checked the oven to see how the corn bread was doing.

"Some trick. It could have gotten me killed. And then whoever would have thought to have blamed Dewey?"

"Is that what you think happened to James Garmone?"

"I'm not betting against it, Ruth."

With a shrug, she turned her attention to supper. I

went upstairs to my bedroom to change out of my wet clothes and see what room I could make for Abby there.

Ruth and I had just finished washing dishes and were about to retire to the living room to watch *Monday Night Football* when Abby and Daisy arrived. Both with smiles on their faces, Abby carried a suitcase half the size of Texas, Daisy her well-worn tennis ball. I'd already changed the sheets on my bed and made a hole in my closet, so now it was just a matter of lugging Abby's suitcase up the stairs.

"I didn't know what to pack, so I packed everything," Abby said.

"No problem," I said as I gritted my teeth and hopped the suitcase up the first stair.

Soon we were all settled in. With one eye on the television, Ruth was reading her *Smithsonian* magazine, one of the multitude that she subscribed to. Abby and I were watching *Monday Night Football,* and Daisy, bored with the inactivity, was sleeping at our feet. All in all, it was pretty cozy there.

"I'm sorry that I didn't call you this morning," Abby said, as we listened to Frank, Dan, and Al analyze the first half. "But I had an emergency at the hospital and didn't get the chance to look at those bones until this afternoon."

"And?" I said.

"As I thought, they all belong to the same person—I'd say a boy of about ten or eleven, maybe even twelve, but that would be stretching it. And I've found nothing that would either identify him, or tell me what caused his death."

"Which leaves us right back where we started."

"I'm afraid so."

Ruth was listening but didn't let on. I could always tell when her antennae were up.

"So how did your day go?" Abby said.

I told her, which took the lion's share of the third quarter.

"I can't believe that Dewey Clinton tried to kill you," she said.

I could see Ruth nod in agreement.

"I can't believe it either, but he did. Which is why I have to talk to him."

"Tonight?" She hoped not.

I thought about going out into the cold again and decided against it. The chill that I had brought home with me and kept through a long hot shower had just in the last few minutes left.

"First thing in the morning."

Satisfied, Abby allowed herself a smile. "And that note of Doc's makes no sense to me. I thought that you said that James Garmone drowned."

"He did drown. Or at least that's listed as the official cause of death."

"But he couldn't have drowned if there was no water in his lungs," Abby argued.

Again I could see Ruth nod. She was a participant whether she knew it or not.

"I know that," I said. "But he also couldn't have died the way that *Freedom's Voice* said he did, so that brings everything about his death into question."

"Which means what?" Abby said.

"Which means I won't know anything more until I talk to Dewey Clinton."

"Then I'd suggest that you talk to him tonight." Ruth could hold out no longer.

"I don't even know where he is, Ruth. You know that."

"He has to come home sometime."

"True, but I'm not willing to stand out in the cold

waiting for him."

"Suit yourself," she said with a note of disapproval.

"Are you saying that you'd be willing to do it?"

"No. I'm saying that you should be."

As usual, she was right. But as the saying goes, that didn't cut any ice with me. To my later regret, I might add.

CHAPTER 14

I was up before dawn the next morning. Daisy had slept there on the floor beside the couch, so before I left, she and I took a walk into the backyard. While she went about her business, I glanced up at the sky to see if I could tell what the day might bring. The same clear, clean sky as yesterday, whatever that meant.

Dewey Clinton was home. At least his bicycle was parked on its kickstand there where it usually was on his front porch. But Dewey didn't answer my knock.

"Dewey, are you in there?" I said.

If he was, he wasn't saying so.

I turned the front door knob, intending to go on in, but though the door appeared to be unlocked, I couldn't get it to budge.

"Damn it, Dewey!" I yelled. "Barricading yourself in

won't help. You'll have to come out sometime."

As I started around the house, I thought that I caught a glimpse of someone leaving Dewey's backyard by way of the alley. But Dewey's giant burning bush blocked my view, and by the time I reached the alley, the man was gone. It wasn't Dewey, I didn't think, but someone whose gait was familiar.

A screen door separated Dewey's back porch from his back stoop. Through it, which had a basketball-sized hole cut in the screen, I could see about twenty hungry cats waiting for me. I could also see a shovel leaning against the house there inside on the porch. It appeared to have fresh dirt on it.

"Last chance, Dewey!" I said, not wanting to run the cat gauntlet. "Otherwise, I'm coming in."

All that did was stir up the cats, who, thinking that I was their meal on wheels, began to mew and purr, then rub against my legs once I was inside the screen door. Nudging them out of the way proved a lot harder than I counted on. To make matters worse, they were starting to make me feel claustrophobic.

"Anyone for baseball," I said as I reached for the shovel.

Using it to sweep them out of the way, I squeezed in the back door and shut it behind me. I regretted it the moment that I did. The smell of Dewey's house, like the sea of cats on his porch, enveloped me, making it hard for me to breathe.

"Dewey, this has gone on long enough," I said. "Come out from wherever it is that you're hiding."

I stood in Dewey's kitchen, whose green linoleum was strewn with cat litter and dried cat crap that had been scratched out of the four litter boxes, one set in each corner of the kitchen, and there left to lie or to be kicked about by whoever was walking in the kitchen. There were also grease stains on the floor beside the stove, what appeared to be milk spills in front of the refrigerator, and there to one side between the floor register and the sink, a dead cat. A long-haired calico, it had died with its eyes open.

"Dewey, if you're anywhere about, I'm coming into the living room," I said.

I could have saved my breath. Dewey was there all right, but he was dead, hanging from the beam that supported his living room by what turned out to be his clothesline. What Dewey had apparently done was to climb up on his footstool, put his head in his homemade noose, and kick the footstool out from under him. In the process, he had blackened his face and nearly bit off his tongue, which hung by a shred of skin from between his clenched teeth.

I recognized the footstool. It was the one that Dewey had made in his eighth-grade shop class. It was always the first thing that he showed you whenever you came to visit.

There on the floor at Dewey's feet was a note that read:

"I done it. I'm sorry"
—Dewey

He had printed it on the back of a Publishers Clearing House envelope. Though he had no way of knowing it now, he was a finalist for $5,000,000.

Dewey didn't have a phone, so once again I had to squeeze by the cats and go to Myrtle Baker's house to call Ben Bryan. Myrtle was already up and in the process of fixing herself some oatmeal. I got Ben Bryan out of bed.

"Ben, it's Garth. I just found Dewey Clinton dead of an apparent suicide."

"Where are you now?"

"Myrtle Baker's."

"Where is he?"

"At home. Next door."

"I'll be there as soon as I get some clothes on."

"You say that Dewey killed himself?" Myrtle said, as she plopped a handful of raisins into her oatmeal and put the lid back on the pan. From somewhere in her house, I could hear Clarence, her monkey, chattering to himself as he rattled about his cage.

I said, "That's what it looks like. You don't by any chance know when Dewey got home last night, do you?"

"Late. That's all I know. It was after I went to bed."

"When was that?"

"Eleven-thirty. Right after the news. That's when I always go to bed." Myrtle decided that the time had come, so after adding some half-and-half and brown sugar, served herself up a bowl of oatmeal. "You sure you don't want some?" she said. "There's a God's plenty."

"No thanks." I didn't even like oatmeal on my good days.

"You hear or see anything in the night out of the ordinary?" I said.

"No. But once my head hits the pillow, I usually don't stir again until daylight. I've always been that way. Makes for a short night, though, come summer."

"Better than no night at all," I said, thinking about Dewey.

Myrtle ate a spoonful of oatmeal, then said, "You plan on doing some digging? I see you brought your shovel."

I had forgotten all about Dewey's shovel and that I had carried it over there. "It's Dewey's," I said.

"I figured it was by the looks of it."

Examining the shovel, I noticed that I had been right at first glance. Some of the dirt on it had not yet dried.

"Thanks for the use of your phone, Myrtle. If Ben

Bryan comes here first, I'm next door."

"Was Dewey in some kind of trouble?" she asked.

"A whole lot of it by the looks of things. Why?"

"Well, Howdy Heavin came by here late last evening, asking about Dewey. You know, if I'd seen him and all. He seemed sort of agitated to me."

"Agitated in what way?" I asked as Myrtle dived back into her oatmeal.

"You know. Half worried, half mad, the way most of us get when someone doesn't show up when and where he's supposed to."

"Did Howdy happen to mention where Dewey was supposed to be?"

"Up at the market, I think. He was supposed to help Howdy stock a truckload of fresh fruits and vegetables that had come in."

"Thanks, Myrtle."

With Dewey's shovel in hand, I walked over to his backyard to see what I could see. The sun was up by now, Dewey's burning bush a brilliant red, the sky a powder blue. Somewhere to the south, someone's cow was bawling. Far to the east, I could hear the westbound freight's whistle as it approached a crossing, probably Brooks Road. I glanced at the railroad tracks no more than fifty yards away, their steel agleam in the morning sun. In another few minutes, the freight would be rumbling by here. It was sad to think that Dewey wouldn't hear it.

Except for the burning bush and a couple scrub pines, nothing of note grew in Dewey's backyard. All of his leaves, the ones that filled his gutters and painted his roof, came either from the giant sugar maple that grew outside his kitchen window right up next to his house or the giant silver maples that grew along Fickle Road in front of his house.

Sitting under one of the scrub pines next to Dewey's wood house was the small misshapen doghouse that Dewey had made for one of the many dogs that he had taken in over the years. But once they were there, Dewey could never keep them home, so as a result they either ran off or got run over or got shot for being in the wrong place at the wrong time. His cats were a different story, however, since they didn't require the keeping that dogs do. In the words of the scripture, they went forth and multiplied—to Dewey's everlasting delight.

Out next to the alley and just to the south of the burning bush, I found where someone had been digging. The three-by-six plot of freshly turned earth looked alarmingly like the one that I had found behind the orphanage last evening. But today I had a shovel and consequently, no excuse not to dig.

Even before I saw his face, I knew who it was. Eugene Yuill's size fourteen Redwing work boot gave him away. So did his badge and uniform, the .38 Police Special strapped to his side. He hadn't been buried very deep, so it was no trouble to uncover him. Neither had he decomposed as much as he might have because of the cool weather. My problem with Eugene as I looked into his dead grey eyes was to find a reason for it all—the reason why he died, the reason why he was still on the job after midnight on a Wednesday, or even on the job at all. The streets terrified Eugene at night. He should have been home in bed, probably would have been home in bed, if all along I hadn't encouraged him not to let his ghosts get the better of him.

I heard someone honking his horn, panicked momentarily when the earth started shaking under my feet; then the westbound freight slowly rumbled by. I started walking toward Dewey's house just as Ben Bryan got out of his Oldsmobile Eighty-eight. I was surprised to see that he hadn't brought Abby along.

"Dewey's in the house," I said.

"What's the matter with you?" he said, apparently thinking that I should be over the shock of finding Dewey by then.

"Eugene Yuill's buried in Dewey's backyard. Was buried, until I dug him up."

Ben Bryan threw up his hands and just stood there. Like me, he had been hoping for a happy ending for Eugene.

"Where's Abby anyway?" he said for something to say. "I tried her at home, then the hospital, and she wasn't at either place."

"She's at my house. I can give her a call if you'd like."

"I'd like. One body is enough for me to worry about."

While Ben fought his way through Dewey's cats, I went over to Myrtle Baker's house to again use her phone. Myrtle had finished her oatmeal, and she and Clarence were in the living room watching *Good Morning America.* I stood for a moment watching it with them. I didn't know about the rest of the country, but Oakalla, Wisconsin, was having its problems today.

"May I use your phone again, Myrtle?"

"You know where to find it. What's the problem now?"

I told her. She seemed more troubled by that news than Dewey Clinton's suicide.

"Eugene Yuill? *Murdered!*" She almost strangled on the word.

"I'm afraid so, Myrtle. Now, if you'll excuse me."

I got ahold of Ruth, who said that Abby was in the shower, but she would pass the news along to her. I told Ruth that I would call her later with my day's plans.

"It's no surprise about Eugene. But it's still a shock," she said.

"For both of us, Ruth. Not to mention Dewey."

"How are you doing?"

"Not very well at the moment."

"Well, hang in there."

"I'm trying to."

As I hung up, I was glad that she had been kind enough not to say, "I told you so."

The thought of facing Dewey's cats again almost sickened me. I was truly tempted to clear them out with the shovel, and if a few got their heads bashed in the process, so be it. But to my relief, Ben had thought to feed them in the meantime, so I only had to kick a couple out of the way before I went inside.

"Why do you figure he barricaded himself in?" Ben asked when I made my way to the living room.

For the first time, I noticed Dewey's couch in front of the door. A heavy dark-green castoff from the 1930s, the couch had bald spots on it where most of its nap had been worn away to bare fabric. Except for the footstool and a small black-and-white TV sitting on an apple crate, the couch was the only furniture in the room. Unless I counted Dewey's wood stove.

"Maybe he didn't want anyone to stop him," I said.

"Figures," Ben said. "You going to help me get him down?"

"Since you asked."

It was a struggle, but we finally got Dewey down after Ben used his pocket knife to cut the clothesline. I now smelled like Dewey, who smelled like stale urine, but I supposed that over the course of the day I'd get used to it.

Dewey was on his back, looking up at us. Even in death, he appeared perplexed by it all, as if he still couldn't quite understand the bum hand that life had dealt him. Neither could I, but then again nobody asked me.

"Help me move the couch," Ben said to get me moving. "I'm not wading through those damn cats again."

I helped him move the couch away from the door. We then opened the door and left it open.

"Did Dewey by any chance leave a note?" Ben asked.

I handed him the Publishers Clearing House envelope.

"Done what?" Ben said as he handed the envelope back to me.

"Killed Eugene Yuill for one thing. Who knows what else?"

Ben Bryan was as angry as I'd ever seen him. "You don't believe that for a minute, Garth, any more than I do."

I started for Dewey's bedroom, the one remaining room in the house besides his bathroom that I hadn't been in so far that day. "Whether we believe it or not, I bet that's what the evidence will show."

"Where are you going?" Ben asked. "I thought you said Eugene was out back?"

"He is. I'm going to look for Doc's memoirs. They should be here somewhere."

"You don't believe that either," Ben said, disgruntled with me.

"If I didn't believe it, I wouldn't be looking."

Ben went outside. I went into Dewey's bedroom, which had a box spring and mattress on the floor, but no bed; a wooden chest of drawers that held only some well-worn jockey shorts, a couple pairs of socks, and some miniature cars and matchbooks that apparently Dewey had collected over the years; and a closet where Dewey's hooded black sweatshirt, stocking cap, and an extra pair of bib overalls hung. The bib overalls looked and felt like new, were in fact new, since I found all of the tags still on them. But who knew how long they had been hanging in Dewey's closet?

Doc's memoirs weren't in plain sight where I had expected them to be, so I tore apart Dewey's bedding looking for them. Evidently no one had ever told Dewey not to eat crackers in bed. I found enough crumbs there to stuff a turkey. But not Doc's memoirs.

On my way out, I met Abby on her way in the front door. "Leaving so soon?" she said.

"I need some air. You'll see why in a moment."

She was staring at Dewey's body on the floor. "I already see why."

Today Abby wore charcoal-grey jeans, a pea-green sweater that matched the green in her blue-green eyes, and a green ribbon that she had used to tie back her hair. She also looked and smelled freshly scrubbed, something that I couldn't say for me.

"You planning on sticking around?" she asked as she slipped a smock over her clothes and put on a pair of plastic gloves. All business now, she had put on her game face as well.

"No longer than I have to," I said. "Call me when you have something."

"You'll be the first. Oh, and Garth?" Her eyes were warmly lit with what I took for love. "Thank you for last night. It was almost like being home again."

"You're welcome," I said, then went out the front door and around back in search of Ben Bryan, who stood beside Eugene's shallow grave.

"You find Doc's memoirs?" he asked.

His back was to Eugene. Apparently he'd seen all that he needed to.

"No."

"I didn't think so."

"But they should have been there, Ben. By all logic."

"That's because you want to pin all of this on Dewey

and have it over with."

"No. It's because Dewey tried to drop Plymouth Rock on my head yesterday."

"Then somebody must have put him up to it," Ben said in Dewey's defense.

"My point exactly," I said then left.

"Where will you be?" Ben yelled after me.

I stopped under Dewey's giant sugar maple. I could see sky through some of its branches, something that I couldn't have done the week before.

"At my office. Probably all day or most of it."

"I'll give you a call," Ben said.

The maple's leaves were a thick amber carpet beneath my feet. How long had it been, I wondered, since I'd had my very own pile of leaves to run and jump in?

"Was there something else, Garth?"

The sound of Ben's voice brought me back again. "Yes. I want to know how that cat in Dewey's kitchen died."

"I'm not a veterinarian, Garth." Ben didn't much like the idea.

"No. But you're a pathologist. I'm sure you're qualified."

"As if I didn't have enough to do," Ben muttered—loudly enough for me to be sure to hear.

CHAPTER 15

The walk to Howard and Elizabeth Heavin's house was a pleasant one. Still morning cool where the sun had yet to find it, the air had that rich October smell of leaf, earth, and frost. And Oakalla itself, in the midst of autumn haze and wood smoke, was starting to awaken, to yawn and stretch and send its citizens out into the streets to earn their daily bread. I knew almost every car by sight and everyone who waved at me. Had it been another day, I might have felt like waving back.

Howard and Elizabeth Heavin sat at their kitchen table, each with a cup of coffee in hand. I had to wonder, especially since I felt the same tension in the air between them, how far they had moved since I last saw them.

"Is Howdy up?" I said.

Elizabeth looked at Howard. Howard shook his head. "Not yet. He spent most of last night at the store. What time was it, Mother, when he got in?"

"I said I'm not your mother," Elizabeth said.

"For God's sake, Elizabeth. It's just a habit. I don't mean anything by it."

Elizabeth's face softened. It was obvious that she loved Howard in spite of whatever disagreement they were having. "I know you don't, Howard. It's just that. . ." She let her hands drop in resignation. "Oh, what's the use? I'm going outside and rake leaves."

"You did that yesterday," Howard said. "And the day before. How many leaves can there be left?"

"I don't know, but if there's one, I'll find it."

She rose from the table and went into their garage. A moment later, I heard its outside door slam.

Howard's eyes were red and sad, as he said, "Can't blame her none. I just wish she'd leave some for me."

"For all our sakes, Howard, go back to work," I said. "Even Howdy would probably welcome it by now."

"What would I welcome?"

Howdy Heavin came into the kitchen wearing blue-and-white striped flannel pajamas and the look of someone who had just stepped off the red-eye special. Even his voice had gravel in it. Meanwhile Howard picked up his coffee and headed for parts unknown.

"I said you'd probably welcome your dad's help in the store by now."

"You got that right." Howdy poured himself a cup of coffee then sat down in the chair across from me. "I'm about to the end of my rope, Garth. But the folks seem determined to let me fall on my face."

"And whose fault is that?"

"Mine, I'm afraid. I was pretty cocksure when I came

back here. I didn't want nor need their help. No sir, not Howdy Heavin." If there was one thing besides soldiering that Howdy *was* good at, it was feeling sorry for himself.

"Why did you come back, Howdy?" It was a question that I felt needed answering.

Howdy scratched his chest as he thought it over. He was so far down that even his mustache seemed to droop.

"I don't know, Garth. The folks said they needed the help, and I needed someplace to go. I was about to lose my base out in California, and there was a lot of pressure on me to retire. Downsizing is what the air force calls it, now that the Cold War is over." Howdy's eyes showed anger as he thought about it. "I suppose I could have fought it, but in the end I would have lost. So I got out and came home."

"To your everlasting regret?"

"Yes and no, Garth. It's good to be home again. But not to be running a grocery store."

"So what are you going to do?"

"I don't know. I'll have to think about it." A change came over him as his back stiffened and the soldier in him took over. Howdy Heavin was back in command. "But you're not here to talk about me."

"No, Howdy, I'm not here to talk about you. Dewey Clinton killed himself last night. I wondered if you knew why."

Howdy's eyes bounced from me to the wall and back to me again. "He did *what?* Where? How?"

"*Why* is what I'm asking. Was Dewey in any kind of trouble that you know of?"

After taking a moment to compose himself, Howdy said, "You're the one who should be answering that question."

"I don't understand."

Howdy finally found his focus. His eyes bore into

mine with an anger that I had a hard time facing. "I think you do, Garth. Dewey was afraid of you for some reason. Terrified is the better word."

"Why?"

"He didn't say. Only that he had done a bad thing and you were going to get him for it."

"Why me? Why not someone else?"

"Because Dewey thought you were the smartest man alive. He thought you could see into his very soul."

"Dewey's words?" Of that I had my doubts.

"My words, Garth. Dewey's thoughts."

"You know better, Howdy."

"I might. Dewey didn't."

"So you're saying that Dewey killed himself because of me?"

"I can't make it any plainer than that."

Howdy was trying to make me assume a guilt I didn't feel. I wondered what his angle was, what he himself was trying to hide.

"The word is that you were looking for Dewey last night. Did you find him?" I said.

"God, Garth, don't you ever let up?" Howdy's anger flared as the red of his face matched the red of his hair. "Isn't it enough that Dewey's dead? Why can't you let it end there?"

"Why don't you tell me why I should?" I said, not backing down. Either I was right or I was wrong, and being a coward about it wasn't going to change anything.

"Because. . ." Howdy's anger began to fade along with the red in his face. "Damn it, Garth, do I have to spell it out for you? I was with Dewey last night. Part of the night anyway."

I smiled inwardly and confidently leaned back in my chair as if I showed aces over kings and held an ace kicker in the hole. To his credit, Howdy was quick to see his mistake.

"Hell, I might as well tell you all of it. You're going to find out anyway. Dewey came by the store early yesterday afternoon, wanting me to go bicycle riding with him. It's something we do. . ." Howdy lost his voice and had to stop for a moment before he could go on. ". . . *did* that we both enjoyed. A holdover, I guess, from when we were kids."

"I thought Dewey was several years older than you?"

"Only four. But four or forty, what difference did it make with Dewey? He was a kid all of his life."

He'd made his point. "Go on," I said.

"I told Dewey that I couldn't go with him, that I had a shipment of fresh produce coming in, and I didn't know when. And I was short-handed anyway because my stock boy had quit on Saturday, so I was going to have to stock it myself. He'd help, Dewey said." Howdy smiled. "Bless him, that was Dewey's way. He'd help. Then everything would be okay."

"So against your better judgment, you went bicycle riding with him?" I said to keep us on track.

"Out to Wildwood Bridge. Dewey said he wanted to show me where he used to live. Except. . ." Howdy looked bewildered, as if unprepared for what had followed. ". . . he didn't stop there where he said his house used to be. He went racing right to the bridge instead. There he jumped off his bicycle and ran to the side, where he could look out over the water. 'I done it, Howdy!' he shouted. 'I done it!' Did what? I asked. 'Killed that fisherman,' he said."

"Are you sure he said *fisherman?*" I interrupted.

Howdy thought it over. "I'd almost swear he did."

Thud! I could almost hear the nail going into Dewey's coffin. "What happened then?" I said.

"Nothing. I told him that he was talking crazy, and I

wasn't going to hear any more of it. To get back on his bicycle and follow me."

"Which he did?"

"Eventually. When he saw that I meant business. We went on across the bridge, up the hill, and just kept on going for who knows how long. I know the sun was well on its way down when we started back."

"You didn't stop at the orphanage?" Which was where I thought I felt someone watching me.

"What orphanage?"

"There at the top of the hill east of the bridge."

Howdy looked puzzled. "I'm sorry, Garth. I don't know what you're talking about."

"Never mind," I said. "I'll figure it out later."

Anyway," Howdy continued, "we were on our way back home when we saw your car parked there east of the bridge and then you walking along the creek toward us. 'Let's scare him,' Dewey said. 'For what he did to me.' 'You scare him,' I said. 'I'm going home.'"

The pupils of Howdy's eyes grew as big as a cat's, as if he were still in shock over what happened next. "I went on ahead, thinking that Dewey would follow. When he didn't, I stopped to see what he was up to. That's when I saw him drop the rock off the bridge. It couldn't have missed you by more than a couple of inches."

"If that," I said.

"I panicked after that happened. I took off riding up the hill as fast as I could go. But I hadn't gone very far when I stopped. If you by chance had caught him, I couldn't very well let Dewey face the music alone. Esprit de corps and all that," he seemed embarrassed to add.

"Before that, you didn't send Jessie down the hill?"

"Jessie?"

"My car."

Howdy gave me a strange look. "Is that what that was making all of that noise? Dewey and I thought it was a deer."

"No chance that Dewey did it?"

"I don't see how, Garth. Dewey and I were on the bridge when it happened."

Which meant, if Howdy was telling the truth, and I had no reason to believe that he wasn't, that someone else besides Dewey had sent Jessie on her merry way down the hill. Either that or she had done it herself just for spite. Not likely, I thought, as with a chill I remembered how uneasy I had felt there behind the orphanage.

"Is something wrong, Garth?" Howdy asked.

"Yes, but I'll get over it. What happened once you stopped to wait for Dewey?"

"He caught up to me a couple minutes later. Before I even thought about what I was doing, I started yelling at him, asking him if he was crazy and what the hell was going on. Then I told him to get out of my sight. I was sick of him." Regret showed in Howdy's eyes. "The only real friend I ever had and I treated him like a dog. Dewey hung his head and started back toward town. I followed a few minutes later."

"Then started having second thoughts?"

"Not until I got back to town and couldn't find him. Then I started worrying about what he might do. I was really relieved when he showed up at the store later on."

"What time was that? Do you remember?"

"After ten because that's when I gave up looking for him. He wasn't there very long. He just stopped by to say he was sorry, he said. And that it wouldn't happen again. I said that as long as he was there, why didn't he give me some help? He couldn't, he said. He was supposed to meet somebody later on. But when I asked who, he wouldn't say."

"Did he give you any indication that he might kill himself?" I said.

Howdy shook his head, fighting back tears. "None whatsoever. But you know how Dewey was, Garth. How his mind worked. You never knew from one minute to the next what he was liable to say or do."

"Do you think that he really intended to meet with someone?"

"I don't know, Garth. Something had him riled, that's all I can say. And it seemed to start that night up at the Corner Bar and Grill. You know, when Dub Bennett was teasing him about the body he'd found."

"Do you think that Dewey ever really found a body?" Two, if I took Dewey's word for it.

"Dewey claimed he did. But I have my doubts."

"Why? Was Dewey in the habit of lying?"

Howdy thought that over then said, "On the contrary, Dewey was the most honest person I've ever known."

"Food for thought," I said.

"I guess you're right," Howdy reluctantly admitted. I was almost to the door when he said, "I blame myself for Dewey's death. Once I had him there, I never should have let him leave the store. Not after yelling at him, like I'd done earlier."

"We all share the blame for Dewey, if there is blame to share. But sometimes, too, God's gun misfires. We can't blame ourselves for that."

"Maybe we should blame God, then. Some people just never have a chance in life."

I didn't try to argue with him. In convincing him that he was wrong, I would have had to convince myself that I was right. And that would have been the far, far harder argument.

Once at my office, I had some serious mulling to do

before I would ever be ready to work. I believed that Dewey had, in fact, "done it." Either he had accidentally killed James Garmone or believed that he had, which amounted to the same thing. He probably hadn't done it on his own, which meant that someone else had put him up to it, and that person in all likelihood had killed Doc Airhart for his memoirs and Eugene Yuill for catching him in the act of killing Doc, since I was convinced they both died on the same night. Or more likely, for stopping him on the street afterwards and then getting bashed on the head. A stranger never would have gotten that close to Eugene—not at night on the street—so it had to be someone that Eugene knew and trusted, which was no help because that included most of Oakalla.

It followed then that whoever had killed Eugene had hidden his body somewhere, then after he had convinced Dewey to kill himself for having "done it," buried Eugene's body in Dewey's backyard; or better yet, somehow persuaded Dewey to bury Eugene in his backyard, then convinced Dewey to kill himself. Dewey was the perfect fall guy—not very bright, yet with a conscience. So he was more than willing to take the blame for any real or imaginary wrongs.

What bothered me, however, about that scenario was that Doc's memoirs were still missing. I should have found them there at Dewey's house, and thus they would pin Doc's murder on Dewey as well as Eugene's. By all logic, they should have been there. There was no reason for them not to have been, unless they implicated someone else besides Dewey in James Garmone's death. And who was it that I saw leaving Dewey's yard as I arrived? Was it the killer himself or some other player in the game?

Laying all of that aside for a moment, I concentrated on the one overriding question of not where, but *if* I went on from here. Apparently the killer would be satisfied to sit tight at this point. Had I been he, I would have been. With Dewey's suicide and Eugene's body in Dewey's backyard and nobody left alive to put the blame on him, all of his tracks were covered, and he could quietly slide back into whatever hole he had crawled out of, and nobody would be the wiser. Justice wouldn't be served, but peace would reign once more in Oakalla, and I could get on with things, the gist of which was running a newspaper. If on the other hand I chose not to look the other way and kept the waters stirred, I might endanger me and mine and lose someone else I loved.

No small bargain, peace. It enabled you to pursue your own happiness, allowed you the luxury (if the fates saw fit) of a long and leisurely life. Without it, civilization was not possible. But without justice and the passion for it, peace was not possible and became just another word for appeasement. I called Ruth.

"Yes, Garth?" she said before I ever told her who it was.

"I need your help. More than ever, it seems."

"You have it. What do you need from me?"

I told her what I knew and what I had decided so far.

"That lets out Howdy Heavin," Ruth said. "If you think that all of this goes back to 1962. He couldn't have been more than twelve years old then."

"You're probably right. But he's still on my list. Unless there's something that you think I should know about him?"

She thought a moment then said, "He's adopted, if you didn't know that. I think he's Elizabeth's sister's boy. She and her husband got killed in a car crash in Oklahoma or some such place, and since Howard and Elizabeth didn't have any children of their own, and weren't likely to, they brought him here to raise."

"How long ago? Since 1962?"

"Years, Garth. That's all I know. He was just a boy when it happened."

"You're right, Ruth. That probably explains a lot of things but nothing that's happened here lately."

"I tried to tell you that."

I glanced outside, saw that the sun was a lot higher than the last time I looked. The day was getting away from me.

"What about Pete Nelson and Milo Thomas? Anything to add to what I already know about them?"

"No. Though Aunt Emma tells me that they went together and sold off both of their woods to buy that prize bull of theirs."

Something teased my brain, said that there was something that I should remember, but though I tried, I couldn't recall it. "Then what am I missing, Ruth, about this whole thing?"

"It sounds like you're missing a euchre player."

"Run that by me again."

"The way you explained it to me, that night at the Corner Bar and Grill when all of this business about 1962 got started, Sniffy Smith came over to talk to you while Dub Bennett, Pete Nelson, and Milo Thomas went into the back room to play euchre. If they did, they played three-handed, unless somebody else was already in there."

I smiled. I could always count on Ruth to set me straight. "You're right, Ruth. Is there any chance that you can find out who that was?"

"I already did. It was Shank Doyle. There's something else that you might as well know, too. That's when Shank bought his sawmill, the fall of 1962."

"After James Garmone was killed in May?"

"That's what my sources say."

"Which proves what?"

"I'm leaving that up to you. Will you be home for

lunch?"

"Probably not. Supper either. It looks like a long day ahead."

"What else is new?" she said then hung up.

CHAPTER 16

I stayed there at my desk, taking phone calls and making notes, and whenever I got the chance, doing a little writing. At times like these, when I was running a day late and a deadline short, I always told myself that I was going to have to hire some permanent help, something that I had been avoiding since I had come to Oakalla. It wasn't that I didn't need the help but the can of worms that would open once another person, then the government, set foot in the door. And given my druthers, I would rather be overworked than wrapped up in red tape.

When I next looked outside again, it was afternoon, and I was as hungry as the proverbial bear. But before I could make good my escape to the Corner Bar and Grill, Danny Palmer pulled up alongside me in his wrecker.

"Ready to go?" he asked.

"Ready to go where?"

"To get Jessie or had you forgotten?"

I had forgotten. "You don't need me to do that."

Danny remained as unflappable as ever, which was why he was such a good businessman. "Probably not. But I do need you to help me dig up that plot of ground behind the orphanage that you were telling me about."

I had no desire to return to the orphanage, with Danny Palmer or anyone else. Besides that, I was hungry.

"I haven't had lunch yet," I protested.

"I brought along sandwiches and a thermos of coffee."

"You haven't eaten yet either?"

"I haven't had a chance."

How, then, could he be so goddamned cheerful? I sighed, seeing no way out. "Let's get going, then. As Frost said, there are miles to go before I sleep."

"Frost? He have a last name?"

"Robert Frost. The poet."

"Oh yeah, the old guy that read the poem at Kennedy's inauguration."

"That wasn't one of his better moments. Poems either."

Danny shrugged. "I guess we all have our bad days."

I nodded. And this was one of mine.

I enjoyed the trip out to Wildwood Bridge more than I thought I would. But with Danny at the wheel, I always seemed to relax and enjoy myself. He exuded a sense of peace and contentment that eluded most of the people I knew. And competence. I always felt safe when I was with Danny, secure in the knowledge that whatever broke, he could fix it—the way with very young eyes I used to look at my father and sometimes, with longing, still did. Also, Danny had brought along two corned beef sandwiches on rye and a thermos of coffee.

"Who's minding the store while you're gone?" I said.

"Sniffy and Dub are taking turns."

"Neither one of them felt their hands fit the shovel?"

Danny gave me a "you know better" smile. "I didn't even ask."

"The sandwiches are good," I said, handing him his. "Who made them?"

"Sharon." Sharon was Danny's wife, the mother of his two children.

"It must be nice."

He smiled. "Yeah, it is."

We had eaten our sandwiches, drunk a round of coffee, and were almost to Wildwood Bridge when he said, "I suppose you heard about Dewey Clinton and Eugene Yuill?"

"Yeah, I was there."

"What do you suppose got into Dewey anyway?"

"I think the better question is, what had Dewey gotten himself into?"

"Any ideas?"

I shrugged. "A couple. But neither makes much sense right now."

We stopped in the middle of Wildwood Bridge. Danny seemed in no hurry to get to the other side where Jessie was.

"Speaking of things that make no sense," he said. "I could've sworn that I saw Eugene out patrolling in his car last night."

Whether it was what Danny said or where he happened to say it, I didn't know, but Wildwood Bridge suddenly started to narrow, squeezing my chest as it did. "Do you mind pulling on through?" I said. "I'm claustrophobic."

"Sorry, Garth. I forgot."

Danny pulled on through the bridge, out into the daylight, and backed into the lane where I'd parked Jessie the evening before. "How's that?" he said.

"Better. Go on with what you were saying."

"There's not much more to it. After the board meeting, I came back to the Marathon to try to get that clutch in Eugene's feed truck because that's the only time I can get any big jobs done, when no one else is around. Anyway, I'm about to close up shop when I see what I swear is Eugene's patrol car cross Jackson Street and head north on Fair Haven Road. Thank God! That was my first thought. Thank God Eugene's still alive and back on the job."

"You're sure it was Eugene's patrol car? After all, you were working on his grain truck. He might have been on your mind."

"Wishful thinking, you mean?"

"Something like that."

His look said that he'd already considered that possibility and dismissed it. "I think I know what I saw, Garth."

"Did you see where the car went from there?"

"No, I'm sorry to say. I was dead tired. All I cared about was that Eugene was alive, and I was finally going home."

"It wasn't Eugene," I said.

"I don't see how it could have been either. Still. . ." He shrugged. "Stranger things have happened around Oakalla."

I got out of the wrecker and filled my lungs with fresh air. I didn't need him to remind me of that.

While Danny worked the lever, I dragged the cable down the hill to where Jessie had come to a stop. Nothing had harmed her in the night. The only change I saw was the layer of leaves that now covered her hood. Fall, in the true sense of the word, was upon us now.

After I'd secured the cable around Jessie's sturdy bumper, her best attribute, and given Danny the go-ahead signal, I walked down along Pine Creek to the gravel bar below Wildwood Bridge. Once again, I stripped down to my boxer shorts and went into the water.

Perhaps Howdy Heavin and I were both wrong and what Dewey had really dropped off the bridge was a giant water-balloon or a hedge apple that he had picked up alongside the road. I entertained that happy thought until I stubbed my toe on a large chunk of limestone that looked exactly like those used as fill alongside the bridge to keep the bank from eroding. Lifting it chest high, I used the old two-handed push-pass to give it a ride out to deep water. There, at least, nobody would trip over it.

That done, I dressed and made my way back up to the road where Danny already had secured Jessie to his wrecker. "You can drive her home, if you like," he said. "I don't think she's hurt any."

"Thanks, but no thanks," I said. "You take her on up to the station. I'll pick her up there later."

"You don't trust her to get you home?"

"That's it. I don't trust her to get me home." Not with almost a full day to plot her revenge.

"Where to now?" Danny said.

"On up the hill to the orphanage, if you don't mind walking."

"I don't mind, but why don't we drive up there?"

"Then we'd have to turn around. Which won't prove easy with Jessie on the back of the wrecker."

"Your point is well taken," he said, as he reached into the wrecker for a couple shovels, handing one to me.

The orphanage looked no more inviting to me in full daylight than it had in yesterday's dusk. Even Danny's presence didn't help any. In fact, it seemed, by its very appearance, to darken his own mood a little.

"Hell of a place to spend your childhood," he said as he stared at the concrete lions, who seemed to have grown in the night.

"That's what I was thinking."

On our way around the orphanage, I was so intent on watching my step and staying out of the briers that I nearly ran into the fire escape. It wasn't the traditional set of open steps but an enclosed metal tube that led up to a third floor window and had what appeared to be a thread from someone's jeans caught on a piece of rust inside its otherwise brightly polished chute. That the thread had survived for twenty or so years seemed a minor miracle to me. "What do you think?" I said, showing the thread to Danny.

"I think the sooner we get out of here the better. This place gives me the creeps."

"Pretty setting, though," I said, as I glanced up at the maples, oaks, and poplars that surrounded it.

Danny wasn't impressed. "If you like trees."

More leaves had fallen in the night, so once again we had to locate the soft patch of ground then clear the leaves from it. As we began to dig, I once more felt my nape start to tingle. A reflex action, I knew, left over from yesterday. But it was still unnerving.

"I don't think we're going to find anything," Danny said after we'd gone down a couple feet and come up empty.

"Let's dig to hard ground at least. It can't be much farther down."

I was wrong. We were at three feet or beyond when my shovel hit its first root. That was all the incentive I needed to call a halt.

"At least we had to try," I said as I took Danny's shovel so that he could climb out of the hole.

He didn't even bother to answer. He'd lost his cheery countenance many shovelfuls ago.

"You ready to leave?" he said.

"In a minute. I'd like to take a look inside first."

"Why, for God's sake?"

I glanced up at the third-floor window that overlooked the plot of ground where we stood. If someone *had* been watching me yesterday, it would have been the perfect vantage point.

"You can stay outside if you like. I won't be long," I said.

"Give me your shovel. I'll be in the wrecker."

It was with a sense of apprehension that I handed over my shovel to him. Now I'd have to go into the orphanage unarmed.

"If I'm not there within fifteen minutes, come looking," I said.

"I'll give you a half-hour," he said, just to be cruel.

The orphanage had a back stairway that by my calculations led all the way to the third floor. Littered with bird and mouse droppings, dead leaves and mud from fallen wasp nests, the stairway didn't appear to show any recent traffic, but the way the wind whistled through there, stirring things up, it was hard to tell. Once I thought I heard a child laughing, but when I stopped, he stopped. Only my imagination, I told myself. Only my imagination.

The stairway led into what was once a dormitory with several iron bunk beds still lined up one after the other along the east wall, two white overhead light sockets at either end of the dormitory, and a dark-stained wooden floor that unlike the stairs, showed recent scuff marks in its dust. The bunk beds numbered ten, so at full capacity the orphanage would have held twenty kids. That is, if all slept there in the dormitory, which I was willing to bet they did, boys and girls alike.

The charred sprig of grapevine took me by surprise because it was on the sill of the window that directly overlooked the patch of broken earth below. Grapevine was what kids used to smoke when they were trying to be bad—at eight or ten before cigarettes came along. Now they smoked grass and crack and didn't have to try to be bad.

I'd overstayed my welcome. The chill running up and down my spine told me so. So did the lengthening shadows, which had begun to overtake the orphanage. But before I left, there was something that I had to do, just to prove to myself that I could. I closed my eyes, and with what only could be described as a leap of faith, went down the fire escape. I'd had better rides in my life, faster slides, more chills and thrills, but none that ever gave me more satisfaction. Or more relief once I opened my eyes and saw daylight again. Had I gotten stuck in there, had I found myself wedged shoehorn tight in that narrow tube, I didn't know what I would have done. But that was the best part of surviving something foolhardy. You didn't have to know.

Our ride back to Oakalla was a quiet one. Danny had his own thoughts. I had mine.

"Do me a favor, will you?" I said as he pulled up alongside the long low concrete-block building that housed the *Oakalla Reporter.* "On your way up Gas Line Road stop at Eugene Yuill's and disable his patrol car. Nothing serious, but nothing obvious."

"If you'll tell me why?"

"A precaution. In case Eugene decides to take a midnight ride again."

"If he does, he won't need his patrol car, Garth."

Suddenly I felt very tired, very sad, as reality set in once more. "To his everlasting delight."

CHAPTER 17

I stopped at my office only long enough to drink a glass of water before I went in search of Pete Nelson. He was outside in his yard, raking and burning leaves. In the yard next to him, Milo Thomas was also raking and burning leaves. I could have talked to both of them at once if I'd wanted, but that only would have complicated matters.

Pete and Milo. Mutt and Jeff, as they were sometimes called by the older residents of Oakalla. Pete was tall, lean, and tanned with snowy-white muttonchops for sideburns and a head of puffy white hair that always reminded me of a snowball bush. Milo was short, round, and bald with thin black eyebrows that looked as if they had been penciled on and a shiny pink scalp that always appeared sunburned, even in January. And while Pete had the long sure stride of a Southern plantation owner and seemed purposeful even in repose, Milo's steps were short and jerky, and he always seemed to be on the run, trying to catch up to himself.

But of the two, I didn't know which one was the better actor. Although Pete appeared the aristocrat and Milo the court jester, Pete was like most modern furniture, all veneer and liable to crack under pressure, as I'd witnessed over the stretch of several money euchre games in the back room of the Corner Bar and Grill. Milo, on the other hand, while he had you distracted, laughing at his crazy antics, managed to play his cards with unerring accuracy. So often at the end of the game, as you stared at the pot that only moments before was seemingly yours for the taking, you saw Milo's fat little hands close around it.

"Afternoon, Pete," I said, standing upwind of his fire. Though I loved the smell of burning leaves, Ruth didn't approve when I wore it home.

"Afternoon, Garth." Pete wore cowboy boots, jeans, and a checkered red-and-black wool shirt that went well with his muttonchops. He offered me a smile that quickly faded. "Terrible thing about Dewey Clinton and Eugene Yuill. Eugene used to haul my feed for me."

"Yes, it *was* a terrible thing," I agreed. "That's why I'm here."

Pete suddenly saw some leaves he'd missed at the far end of his yard. I followed him there.

"Garth, I've got nothing to say on the matter. So you might as well go on about your business," Pete said.

"You're not feeling guilty, are you, Pete?"

"No! I'm not feeling guilty." He swallowed hard as I watched his Adam's apple bob up and down. "It's just that I know how you are. When you zero in on somebody, bad things seem to happen to him."

"Only if he's done something wrong," I said.

Pete began to rake furiously at the leaves, digging up grass and dirt as well. "And I said for you to mind your own business."

"Just tell me why you and Milo came in separate cars from your wives then left Doc's funeral early."

He started to deny it then thought better of it. "We came in separate cars because our wives wanted to go shopping up at Stevens Point after the service, and Milo and I didn't want to go along. As for leaving the service early, we figured we'd heard enough out of you for one day."

I let that pass, knowing that it came with the territory. "Then you won't mind telling me where you went," I said.

"Yes, I do mind," Pete said. "But I don't mind telling you where to go."

He continued to move about his yard, looking for leaves. I continued to follow him.

"Let's jump back a few years, then," I said. "To 1962. Wasn't that the year you and Milo bought your prize bull?"

"What of it?" He was now working a small pile of leaves across his yard toward the fire.

"I was wondering where you got the money for it?"

He stopped raking long enough to glance in Milo's direction. It looked to me like a plea for help.

"Where do you think we got it? We borrowed it."

"I heard you each sold the timber off your land and then used that money to buy your bull."

Pete resumed raking. "That's right. We did."

"Then which is it, Pete?"

"Ask Milo. He's the one with the memory."

"Ask Milo what?" Carrying his rake and wearing a baggy blue sweatshirt over his baggy black slacks, Milo Thomas had wandered over to where we stood. Pete seemed to sag in relief, as the tension left his face and his ever-ready smile returned.

"Where we got the money to buy that prize bull all those years ago," Pete said in answer to Milo's question.

"Well, Garth," Milo said slowly, appearing as genial as ever, "I would reckon that's our business."

Though he then added a smile, Milo's eyes weren't smiling. A metallic grey, they had the hard steely look of ball bearings.

I said, "It probably is your business, Milo, but I can probably find out if I decide to dig deep enough."

"And why would you want to do that?"

Feeling a cold breeze, I glanced to the west where the sun was about to set. It had been a beautiful day, what I had seen of it.

"I'm investigating a murder, Milo, a couple of them in fact, and I believe they both might lead back to 1962 and you."

When Milo smiled broadly, as he was doing now, you could see the dark stains on his teeth from years of chewing tobacco and that about every other tooth was missing. "Garth, I've heard it all in my day, but that about takes the cake. What could anything that we did or didn't do all that long ago have to do with anybody's murder? And if you're talking about Eugene Yuill, I hear Dewey Clinton's already confessed to that."

"Then why your interest in Doc's memoirs?" I said. "Nineteen sixty-two in particular?"

Milo looked at Pete in mock confusion. "What in the hell is he talking about, Pete? You have any idea?"

All Pete could do was shake his head and give us a mindless grin. Evidently he didn't trust himself to speak.

"*What* is in those memoirs, Garth?" Milo was still smiling. "When you can tell us that, we might be more inclined to talk to you. Until then, it might be best for you and yours if you stick to running your newspaper."

No fool I, I knew a threat when I heard one.

"And as far as that badge you're carrying," Milo continued, "it doesn't make you the law in Oakalla any more than living here in the middle of town makes me the mayor. So you know what you can do with it."

I eased my hand out of my back pocket where my billfold was. I *was* just about to flash my special deputy's badge to show him I meant business.

"If you've broken the law, Milo, then you'll find out how much weight that badge carries."

"Yeah, yeah, tell me another one."

Then I felt the presence of someone behind me as the bully look on Milo's face ran in search of somewhere to hide. Only one person in Oakalla that I knew had that effect on people.

"Hello, Rupert," I said without turning around.

"Evening, Garth," Rupert said. "Pete, Milo, how are you boys doing?"

Both managed to offer a greeting, though neither was either very loud or heartfelt.

"We were just talking about the law in Oakalla," I said to Rupert. "And whether that badge you gave me means anything or not."

"Who said it didn't?" Though Rupert spoke slowly, softly, as was his custom, there was no mistaking the cold glint in his eye for anything but what it was. The law, which he had ruthlessly upheld during his reign as sheriff, was something that was not open to debate.

"Aw hell, Garth, we were just kidding you," Milo said with a smile. "Weren't we, Pete?"

"Just kidding," Pete said, finding his voice again. "We like to give Garth here a hard time."

"No harm, no foul," I said for their benefit, though

none of us there believed it.

"Well, I've got leaves to rake," Milo said. "So if you gents will excuse me. . ." He headed back home.

"Same here." Pete make a beeline for his backyard, leaving Rupert and me by the pile of burning leaves.

"Feels good," Rupert said as he knelt to warm his hands. Then he rose and turned to warm his backside. "From the looks of it, things weren't going your way a minute ago. But then they haven't gone your way much lately." It wasn't a question. I wondered how he knew.

"Right on both counts. I could still use your help, if it's available?"

He didn't even consider it. "Sorry, Garth. You're going to have to ride this one out yourself. Elvira and I leave for Texas day after tomorrow."

"What about Doc's memoirs?"

"What about them?"

"You said that you were going to help me look for them."

"I have looked for them."

"And?" I said, when he didn't continue.

"And I don't think that they can be found. At least not where they are now."

"Where are they now, you have any idea?" The look on his face said he did.

"Some. But it'll take a search warrant."

"I'll get you one."

He shook his head. "No. If we're patient and play our cards right, they're more likely to turn up than if we go charging in with our guns blazing."

"Says you," I said, disappointed in him. "You're headed for Texas in two days."

"You've survived without me before."

"Barely," I said, sincerely meaning it.

He put his hand on my shoulder. It was a rough gnarled hand, with a lot of strength in it. "Take heart, Garth. The battle's not been lost yet."

I glanced from Pete to Milo, each of whom had done more gawking than raking since leaving us. "They're stonewalling me, Rupert. They're guilty of something. I just don't know what."

"Perhaps with a little more thought, you will," he said as he dropped his hand and started to walk away.

"One question, Rupert," I said, bringing him to a halt. "Why? Why won't you put your badge back on just this one last time? I know Doc would do the same for you."

Rupert remained standing with his back to me. I wished that he would turn around so that I could at least try to read his face.

"Because if I ever put it back on, I'm not sure I could take it off again."

"What would be the harm in that?"

"I'm an old man, Garth, or haven't you noticed?"

I hadn't wanted to notice. "You still command the same respect you always did. Look what happened here this evening."

Rupert turned around. His face showed the agony of a man at war with himself—that of an old chief, who knew that he should now walk in peace, but still remembered, still felt to the bottom of his soul, the rhythm of the war drums, the thrill of taking coup.

"Those two don't count, Garth. What would happen when I met up with some real bad guys?"

He turned and started home. I watched him a moment then headed for the west end of town.

CHAPTER 18

Steven Doyle could only be described as a hard man. The lines of his face were hard, his body was hard, his outlook on life was hard. Lanky, and long-muscle lean, the way Abe Lincoln was before the toils of office wore him thin, Steven Doyle had a white chain-saw scar on his left leg that ran from his ankle to his knee, and he was missing his ring and little fingers on his left hand down to their first knuckles.

Now in his mid-fifties, he had started his career as a timber buyer for the sawmill and lumberyard that he now owned. A bachelor, he was said to have never had time for a wife—or for a courtship, which might have led to a wife. So since he was a hard driver in a hard and dangerous profession, with no one to share his passion or to soften life's blows, it was no wonder that Steven Doyle was a hard man or that everyone who knew him called him Shank.

Though the lumberyard and sawmill were shut down for the evening, and the workers gone home, a light was on in Shank Doyle's office on the second floor of the mill. A wooden stairs led up to it. I climbed the stairs, and when he didn't answer my knock, let myself inside.

"Evening, Shank," I said, offering my hand. "You have a minute?"

He ignored both me and my hand and went on with his paperwork. It was strange to see someone's work desk without at least one photograph or keepsake on it. But Shank's desk was bare of mementos of any kind.

"What is it you want, Ryland? I'm a busy man."

Then he looked up at me, and immediately I found myself wanting to look away. Though they weren't exactly green, neither were Shank's eyes any of its shades that I could name. They looked at me, as they did at all of life, with contempt.

"You know what's happened in Oakalla the past few days?" I said.

Shank went back to his paperwork. I was relieved not to have to face his glare.

"I know we lost a good man in Doc Airhart," he said. "What else is there to know?"

"Did you also know that Eugene Yuill was murdered?"

"I heard that. I also heard that you caught the fool that supposedly did it. Or that he hung himself, saving you the trouble." Shank looked up at me again, his eyes no more friendly than before. "What does that have to do with me?"

"I have reason to believe that Dewey didn't kill Eugene, and that whoever did, also killed Doc for his memoirs."

"Even if that's true, and that's news to me about Doc, I still don't see your point."

Shank glanced at his watch, which like mine was a heavy-duty Timex. Someone once said, Kurt Vonnegut I think, that a watch's life span was inversely proportional to its price. If so, mine should last forever.

"You need to get somewhere?" I said.

"There's a euchre game later. Whenever I get there."

"You, Dub, Pete, and Milo?"

He seemed surprised that I knew. "That's our usual foursome. Why?"

"That was the same foursome that was playing the night that Dewey spouted off about finding the body there below Wildwood Bridge."

"Ryland, you've lost me," Shank said as he shoved his paperwork aside, then leaned back in his chair and clasped his hands behind his head. "But since I can't get any work done with you here, I'll hear you out. One time. No more. Then you'll get the hell out of here, or I'll throw you out. And no more of your Mickey Mouse questions and your beating around the bush. Just tell me what you think you have on me, and I'll tell you if you're right or not. Is that clear?"

"Clear," I said.

"Then let's have it."

"Okay, here's what I think I have on you. Doc's memoirs were ready for 1962, which by your own admission you, Dub, Pete, and Milo were all interested in."

"Not by my own admission. But since you brought it up, I will admit that for my own reasons I *was* interested in them."

I found a chair and sat down. For someone who might have something to hide, Shank Doyle was disarmingly forthright.

I continued, "Nineteen sixty-two also happens to be the year that (1) James Garmone drowned in Pine Creek there below Wildwood Bridge; (2) Pete and Milo bought their prize bull, the one that made their dairy herds; (3) you bought the sawmill and lumberyard from Sam Pingleton. All in that order, I believe. My sources also tell me that Pete and Milo got the money to buy their bull by selling off their timber and that you were the buyer on the deal." I was just guessing about the last part, but it was a good guess.

Shank looked at me with annoyance, yet without the slightest hint of unrest, the way that he might have at an ant that had just crawled across his desk. "You wasted fifteen minutes of my time to tell me that?"

"I'm not done yet."

"Oh yes you are," he said as he rose from his chair.

I was no more afraid of Shank Doyle than I was of any other man, but I did believe that he intended to throw me out on my ear and that I would be powerless to stop him.

"James Garmone was also murdered. I didn't tell you that," I said, having saved what I hoped was my best for last.

"If he was, then that idiot Dewey Clinton was the one who did it," he said.

"How do you know that?"

"I know that because. . . Out!" he ordered, pointing a finger to show me the way.

"I'll be back," I said, just to have the last word.

But it was an empty threat, and Shank Doyle knew it. He sat back down at his desk and began to sort through a stack of papers. He didn't even bother to look up as I left.

CHAPTER 19

After supper at the Corner Bar and Grill, I returned to my office to see what, if anything, I might redeem from the day. It had been a marvelous evening—solemn and still, pink, lavender, and blue, without even a hint of a cloud in the sky—one of those evenings that you wait all year for and then miss because you're in no mood to enjoy it. For the first time in a long time, I felt defeated.

Then Ben Bryan came into my office, looking like I felt. Whoever said misery loves company got it right. Ben Bryan, despite the cloud he brought with him, was a welcome sight.

"You talked to Abby yet?" Ben asked, as he laid Eugene Yuill's .38 Police Special and its holster on my desk.

"What's that for?"

"Eugene doesn't have any more use for it. I figured you might."

I slid Eugene's gun and holster off to one side where I wouldn't have to look at them. "No, to answer your question," I said. "I haven't talked to Abby yet. I haven't seen her since this morning."

"She living with you now?" Either way it was all the same to him.

"Just temporarily, until this is all over."

He pulled up one of the two bentwood chairs that stood against the east wall of my office and sat down. "As far as I'm concerned, it's over now. Everything that I found says that Dewey killed Eugene Yuill."

"As expected."

He sighed in exasperation. "Garth, we found hairs from Dewey's head on Eugene's body. And Dewey's shovel was the one that dug Eugene's grave, and Eugene's bloody night stick was there in the back of Dewey's refrigerator."

"What were you doing in Dewey's refrigerator?"

Ben's look was not kind. "Looking for something to feed those damn cats with. My point is that every bit of physical evidence that we have points to Dewey as Eugene's killer."

"Including Dewey's fingerprints on the shovel and night stick?"

"That goes without saying, though we haven't got that far yet."

"I wish Clarkie was here," I said.

Ben got up and walked over to the shelf where I kept my mugs, hot plate, saucepan, sugar, spoons, creamer, and jar of instant coffee. "I'll pretend I didn't hear that."

"When it came to fingerprints, Clarkie had no equals," I said without apology. "Now we'll have to call somebody in from the outside."

"We're going to have to do that anyway, Garth," Ben said as he spooned some coffee into a mug and poured in the hot water. "We've got a double homicide and a suicide that we're sitting on. Outside help might be welcome at this point, if only for a fresh point of view."

Ben sat back down. I got up to fill my coffee mug.

"And you know what the outside help will say. Dewey killed Eugene and Doc. Case closed."

"Would that be so bad, Garth?"

"It wouldn't be so bad. It just wouldn't be right." Coffee in hand, I returned to my desk. It felt good to rest on something solid. "What happened to change your mind?" I said. "This morning you were ready to defend Dewey to the ends of the earth."

Ben took a sip of his coffee and winced. Since it couldn't have been too hot, he must have made it too strong.

"Maybe I'm just tired is all. I've been at this all day," he said. "And maybe Dewey really did do it. We don't have one shred of evidence that says he didn't."

I took a sip of my coffee and winced. Maybe, after three months, it was time to change the jar.

"We didn't find Doc's missing memoirs," I said.

"That doesn't prove anything, since we don't even know that they're missing for sure. Doc could have hidden them somewhere."

"He could have. I don't think he did."

"Still, Garth, you see what I'm getting at. Instead of some giant conspiracy, maybe Dewey just went bonkers last Wednesday night and killed Doc and Eugene for no reason."

"How likely is that?"

"Based on the evidence, very likely."

"What about his motive? And what about those bones we found in Doc's morgue? Did Abby ever show you those?"

"I looked at them yesterday evening. In fact, they're at my place now."

"And?"

Ben took another sip of coffee, forcing it down. "And they're just what she said they were, the bones of a young boy. Nine, ten, eleven, somewhere in there."

"Can you think of any reason at all why Doc would have kept them hidden down there where he did?"

"No, Garth. Unless he was protecting someone."

"Dewey again?" That appeared to be where we were headed.

Giving up on his coffee, Ben set his mug on the floor. "It stands to reason, Garth. Maybe Dewey really did find two bodies, like you say he claimed he did. And maybe he killed them both. If Doc knew about it, then that would be his motive for killing Doc."

"If it's true that Dewey did kill both of them, why would Doc have sat on it all of this time?"

"If he thought it was an accident, he might have done it to protect Dewey. What would be the point of locking him up if Dewey didn't know any better?"

"To keep him from doing it again."

Ben rose, opened my north window, and threw his coffee out through the screen before returning the mug to the shelf. "It appears to me that's exactly what Doc should have done. But even Doc's judgment wasn't perfect. . ." He found his first smile of the evening. "Though it was close at times."

"What exactly did Eugene die from?" I asked, seeing that he was about to leave.

"A fractured skull, as a result of several blows to the head."

"From his own night stick?"

"Yes."

"That means his killer had to get close to him."

"Very close, Garth. At least within arm's length."

"I was thinking more along the lines of how he managed to get close to him. Eugene never would have allowed that to happen with someone he didn't trust."

"Another feather in Dewey's cap," Ben said, his hand resting on my office door.

"One last thing, Ben. How did the cat die?"

Ben snapped his fingers in anger. "I knew there was something I forgot."

"You didn't do that cat?" I said, disappointed.

"Did the cat," he said. "It died of a broken neck, or strangulation, whichever came first. But that's not what I forgot. Several years ago, I've lost track of how many, somebody in the south end of town took to killing other people's cats. Strangling them, just like that calico in Dewey's kitchen. There was quite a stink about it, and unless I'm mistaken, the finger got pointed at Dewey."

"But did they ever prove that Dewey did it?"

"Not so that I remember. But seeing that dead cat this morning brought it all back again."

"Thanks, Ben. I appreciate all you've done."

"Just doing my job," he said. "Which, by the way, I was hoping to turn over to Abby one of these days soon. Now she's talking about going back for more training. I hope talk is all it is."

"So do I, Ben. But I think she's got her heart set on it."

He shook his head, as if this were the last straw. "Can't blame her none, I guess. Not if she wants to be a real pathologist."

"You're a real pathologist," I said.

Ben dismissed me with a wave of his hand. "I'm a mortician, Garth. Or was. And a damned good one at that. But Doc was the pathologist. He had forgotten more about it than I ever knew. And if Abby stays with it, I think she'll be every bit as good as he was." He forced a smile. "Not that that does either one of us any good, but someday it will be nice to say, we knew her when."

"Yeah," I said without enthusiasm. "I'm sure it will."

"Night, Garth."

"The cats, Ben? Whatever came of it?"

"Nothing. They stopped dying, so it all blew over."

He left, leaving me feeling even more alone.

CHAPTER 20

Three hours later, after scanning five years (1962 to 1967) of *Freedom's Voice,* I had found no mention of the dead cats or no reason why they had suddenly stopped dying. Neither had I accomplished anything of value on that Friday's *Oakalla Reporter,* so I went home.

I had hoped to slip in quietly, find all asleep, and hit the couch for some much-needed rest. Those hopes were dashed when simultaneously I saw the light on in the kitchen and Daisy came bounding up to the front door to greet me.

"We're in here," Ruth said, meaning the kitchen.

I hoped she didn't hear my groan.

As promised, Ruth and Abby were indeed in the kitchen. And if I were to judge by the pile of cigarettes in

Abby's ashtray, they had been holding a council of war there. A council of some kind anyway. But unlike Ben Bryan and me, they showed no sign of defeat, not even a hint of it. On the contrary, they seemed energized, ready to do battle.

"Am I in the wrong house?" I said, as I poured myself a cup of coffee and sat down at the kitchen table. "Or didn't you have the day I did?"

Daisy came over to me and put a paw on my knee, wanting me to scratch her ears. I did, just to keep from feeling guilty.

"I don't know about Ruth, but I probably put in a worse day than you did," Abby said. "At least you didn't have to cut up one of your friends."

"No. But I had to dig him up."

Ruth said, "And I had to hear everybody and his brother tell me about it, so neither one of you is going to get any sympathy from me."

It was a Mexican standoff, Oakalla's version of "anything you can do. . ."

"So what else went wrong today?" Ruth said.

I told them the gist of it then said, "I know Pete, Milo, and Shank are stonewalling me, but I don't know why. It's no crime to sell off your own woods, even if you make a brier patch out of it."

"It is in my book," Abby said.

"Mine, too. But our books don't count."

"And if somebody hadn't cleared the land, we'd all be living in caves and hunting bears for our food," Ruth said.

Tired of having her ears scratched, Daisy went over to lie down at the back door. She looked sad to me, as if she somehow knew that all this was temporary and home would never be the same again. Or maybe I was reading my own thoughts into hers.

"Besides," Ruth continued, "why would James Garmone care whether Pete and Milo cut down their woods or not, and even if he did care, what could he do about it?"

"What if there were an endangered species of some kind in their woods that nobody knew about?" Abby said. "No, on second thought, I doubt that would have mattered back then."

Again something tickled my brain, but I was too tired to pursue it.

"It's not likely," Ruth said. "As I remember it, those farms weren't any prizes when they bought them. Or at least Karl didn't think so." Karl was Ruth's late husband, who had died from lung cancer the year before I moved to Oakalla.

"Not any prizes in what way?" I said.

"They'd pretty well been used up by the time Pete and Milo got ahold of them."

"Their woods, too?"

"I don't know about that. But it stands to reason. Which leads me to wonder about the bull they bought. He couldn't have been worth much, even if they did sell their whole woods to buy him."

"Don't forget Shank Doyle," I said. "I'm sure he got a cut of the deal, too."

"I don't understand," Abby said. "Ruth, are you saying that the money for the bull had to come from somewhere else?"

"It didn't have to. But I feel like it did."

"Why couldn't they have just borrowed the money?" Abby said.

Ruth said, "Because nobody around here with any sense would have loaned it to them. The only thing that Pete Nelson and Milo Thomas ever did right in their lives was to buy that bull, which was the making of them." She paused then said, "I take that back. The other thing they did right was not to sell that bull to Wilmer Wiemer when he offered to buy it the first thing right out of the box."

"It had to be a good bull, then, if Wilmer was interested in it," I said. Wilmer Wiemer, owner of Oakalla Savings and Loan, the Best Deal Real Estate Company, and anything else of value that he could get his hands on, never took any wooden nickels.

"So where did the money come from?" Abby said.

We all looked at each other without an answer. Back to square one.

Abby lighted another cigarette, and I glanced at Ruth to see what her reaction would be. Karl had been a heavy smoker all of his life and had only quit after his lung cancer was diagnosed. Though Ruth said that she didn't blame the cigarettes, I had to wonder. As for me, I didn't mind if Abby smoked. I just didn't want her dying from it.

But Ruth could read me like a book, and her return glance said to mind my own business.

"Did I miss something?" Abby, who had eyes of her own, said.

"Garth was wondering if I minded if you smoked. I don't," Ruth said.

"Because of Karl, he means?" Abby said.

"Yes. Because of Karl."

Now that I had their attention, I said, "The point is that you've both been here at the table for a long time, long enough for Abby to fill an ashtray. I have to wonder why?" It wasn't a perfect escape, but I'd take it under the circumstances.

"Do you want to tell him or should I?" Ruth said.

"I will," Abby volunteered, as she rose to fill her coffee cup, then filled Ruth's while she was up. "Ruth and I have been giving a lot of thought to this," she said on her return to the table. "And we were wondering if perhaps James Garmone didn't drown after all."

"Then who was it that had no water in his lungs?"

"Think, Garth," Ruth said. "Even though it has been a long day."

But try as I might, I couldn't think of anyone. James Garmone, especially with what I now knew about his death, which couldn't have happened as it was written, was the logical candidate for murder.

"I can't think of anyone," I said at last.

"What about the boy whose bones we found?" Abby said.

"What about him?" I still couldn't make the connection.

I looked at Ruth, who was bursting at the seams to tell me, but this was Abby's show, and Ruth would be damned if she would ruin it for her.

"Let's start with an assumption," Abby said. "Let's assume that Dewey Clinton really did find two bodies under Wildwood Bridge, and for argument's sake, let's assume that he really did think that he killed one of them—James Garmone. Let's further assume that he was wrong about that, that he really hadn't killed James Garmone but done something to make it seem as if he had."

"Like dropping a rock on him?"

"That's my first choice," Abby said.

"And mine," Ruth added.

Abby continued. "So while Dewey runs off to tell his parents about what happened, the real killer, or killers, move in and drown James Garmone while he's still in a state of shock."

"There's only one thing wrong with that," I said. "The real killer, or killers, would have had to have been there waiting for Dewey to do whatever he did. Unless they were mind readers, that seems like too much of a coincidence to me."

"Not if they put Dewey up to it."

She had a point. "Go on," I said.

"Unknown to the killer, or *killers,*" she emphasized, "there was a witness. Let's say a boy from the orphanage who had come down to Pine Creek to play."

I felt my skin start to tingle, the way it had outside the orphanage today. But I didn't believe in ghosts.

"What's the matter, cat got your tongue?" Ruth said, using one of her and Grandmother Ryland's favorite expressions.

"It's nothing," I said.

"We'd still like to hear about it."

Abby nodded in agreement. I thought back to the good old days when I only had to deal with one of them at a time.

"I just had a strange experience out at the orphanage today, that's all. It felt like someone was watching me when no one was there."

"Watching you from where?" Ruth said.

"A third-story window in what used to be the dormitory. When I went up there, I saw evidence that someone else had been there before me. A boy, by the looks of it. He had been smoking grapevine and sliding down the fire escape."

In the silence that followed, Daisy's whimper was the only thing that I could hear. She must have been having a bad dream, perhaps about a man with a rubber hose.

"Probably neighborhood kids playing up there," Ruth said.

"That's what I would have thought. Except that there aren't any kids in the neighborhood. Are there, Abby?"

"I didn't see any when we were out there. In fact, I

didn't even see a house in the neighborhood, not one that looked lived in anyway."

"There has to be a logical explanation for it," Ruth said.

"Says she who is psychic."

That put Ruth on the warpath, as I knew it would. "I've never claimed to by psychic, and you know it. Sometimes I see things is all."

"Like the time you saw Diana in a basement? If that wasn't psychic, I don't know what is."

"Diana?" Abby said with more than casual interest. "Who's she?"

Ruth and I exchanged glances. Hers said I'd gotten myself into this, I could get myself out.

"An old friend of mine," I said. "She's living in New Mexico now." I turned to Ruth. "Or is it Arizona?"

"You know darned good and well it's New Mexico. She's an artist out there," Ruth went on to explain to Abby. "Or calls herself one."

"I see," Abby said as the temperature in the kitchen began to plummet. "Was she psychic, too? Or did she have other attributes that I should know about?"

"We'll discuss Diana another time," I said. "In private."

I didn't want to discuss Diana at all, but especially not in front of Ruth, whose perception of Diana Baldwin was vastly different than mine. For her own reasons, Ruth had very little use for Diana. I once had loved her with all of my heart.

"Where were we?" I said.

"Never mind," Abby said. "We can talk about it *another time."*

She started to rise from the table. It was Ruth who came to my rescue, as she put a gentle hand on Abby's shoulder for her to sit down again.

"We were saying that perhaps a boy from the orphanage saw the killer, or killers, drown James Garmone and then got killed by them later because of what he knew," Ruth said.

"If that's the case, then why didn't the killer just drown the boy in Pine Creek, instead of suffocating him, or whatever it was they did to kill him?" I said.

"Did you say suffocate? That's it, Ruth," Abby said, coming back to life. "They could have suffocated him. That's why Ben and I couldn't find a cause of death."

"Just like Doc," I said.

"You're right, Garth. Just like Uncle Bill. And no one would be the wiser."

"Garth's right about another thing, too," Ruth said. "Why not just drown the boy in the creek? Especially if there are two of them, like we think there are."

"Why two of them?" I said. "For that matter, as long as we are complicating things, why not six or ten?"

Ruth was the one who set me straight. "Because dazed or not, James Garmone would have put up a fight if somebody tried to drown him. I don't see how one person by himself could have done it."

"James Garmone was wearing waders, don't forget. That would have put him at a disadvantage."

"Not that much in shallow water, where you say he was standing."

"Sitting is more like it, after getting hit by a rock."

"Still, it would have been hard for one person alone," Ruth argued.

Thinking it over, I agreed with her logic but not necessarily with her conclusion, since my gut feeling said that the killer was working alone. Then there was still the matter of why he suffocated the boy, if he suffocated him, instead of drowning him.

"I don't have an explanation," Abby said when I queried her.

I looked at Ruth. "I don't either," she said. "If they were afraid of somebody seeing them from the road, they could have drowned him somewhere upstream and let his body float down to the bridge."

"Not upstream," I said. "Not very far anyway. With bluffs on both sides, it's too hard to get to."

"Somewhere else, then."

I glanced around the table. Abby looked discouraged, so did Ruth, which made it unanimous.

Abby rose, kissed me on the cheek, and with a "Good night," went upstairs to bed. Ruth then rose, preparing to follow her. Soon, as I'd wished earlier, I'd have the whole house to myself.

"What did I do wrong?" I asked Ruth after I heard my bedroom door close.

"You did nothing wrong, Garth. It's been a long day for all of us."

"Perhaps I shouldn't have mentioned Diana."

"Perhaps you shouldn't have" was all she said.

She made her way to the sink where she dumped out her coffee and rinsed out her cup. Her steps were slow and measured. Weariness had claimed us all right down to the bone.

"A couple things, Ruth, before you turn in. One, I need you to find anybody who might have lived in that orphanage and can tell us if somebody from there disappeared in 1962. Two, what do you know about the cats that were being killed in the south end of Oakalla several years ago?"

"Only that it happened."

"No one was ever caught in the act?"

Ruth took Abby's ashtray from the table and dumped

it into the wastebasket, leaving the ashtray in the sink to be washed in the morning. "I don't know the particulars, Garth. Why don't you look it up in *Freedom's Voice.* That's how I found out about it."

"I tried, but I went from 1962 to 1967 without finding anything."

"Why 1962, besides the obvious?"

"That's when Dewey Clinton moved to town or shortly thereafter."

Ruth looked puzzled.

"Didn't Abby tell you about the dead cat we found in Dewey's kitchen. Someone had strangled it."

Ruth stared at me for the longest time then said, "Check again, then, if it'll ease your mind any."

She went up to bed, leaving Daisy and me alone in the kitchen. "You coming, girl?" I asked Daisy after brushing my teeth.

We went outside, she to do her thing, I to do mine. Overhead, a zillion stars shone down on me as I looked up at them. How great thou art! I thought about the universe. How great thou art! But that didn't make my own problems seem one tiny bit smaller.

CHAPTER 21

The answer came to me in the night. Not *the* answer, who had killed Doc and Eugene and why, but the answer to the question that had been tickling my brain. I nudged Daisy out of the way so that I could get off the couch and made my way to the phone.

"Clarkie, this is Garth. I hope I didn't get you out of bed."

"It wouldn't be the first time," he grumbled.

Clarkie had rented an apartment in Madison now that he was working there. Any day now, I expected his house in Oakalla to come up for sale.

"I have a favor. I suppose you heard about Dewey Clinton and Eugene Yuill?"

"Yeah. Aunt Norma called me last evening. Said Dewey clubbed Eugene to death then hanged himself."

"That's the official version."

Clarkie sighed. His whole purpose in taking the computer job in Madison was to escape Oakalla and its demands on him. Now here he was right back in the middle of it again.

"What's your version of it, Garth?"

"I don't have time to explain it all, Clarkie. But let's just say that I don't buy Dewey as Eugene's killer. Neither do a few of the others here in Oakalla. And what I need from you is a confirmation of that."

"I'm listening."

I told him where I wanted him to go and what I wanted him to do. "There's always the chance that it's not there, and even if it is there, it might not tell us anything. But it's all I have right now."

"I'll see what I can do, Garth." Though he was not at all enthused.

"I hate to drag you into this, but I didn't know where else to turn."

"That's not it, Garth."

"Then what's the problem?" I asked, when he didn't elaborate.

"The problem is, it should have been me, not Eugene. He never was cut out for that sort of work, and you and I both know it."

I bit my tongue and kept my peace. Neither was Clarkie cut out for that sort of work, which was why he was doing what he was doing.

"You can't blame yourself, Clarkie. Eugene knew the risks when he took the job." Actually, as he had once confided to me, Eugene had no idea of the risks involved when he took the deputy's job, though he was soon to learn them.

"I still feel responsible."

"Then help me catch his killer."

"I'd rather be there to do it myself."

I was losing patience with him, which when he was still sheriff was a daily occurrence. "Clarkie, I'm glad you're not here. I'm glad you're where you are—safe, warm, doing what you love to do. I've buried enough of my friends lately."

"I won't let you down, Garth."

"Have you ever?" I hung up.

"What was that all about?" Ruth said as she padded into the kitchen to put the coffee water on.

I told her.

"If you're right, then we've got everything but the reason why they didn't drown the boy from the orphanage. But maybe that will come out in the wash."

"We're still making a lot of assumptions, Ruth. We don't even know that there was a boy from the orphanage."

"Dewey Clinton said there was or the same as, if we're talking two people here. And he's dead now."

She had a point.

I left for work before Abby ever made it downstairs. It was just as well because I didn't quite know what to say to her now that I was on the defensive. My limited experience in these matters said the less I said, the better. Or in his father-in-law's succinct advice to my father on his wedding day, "When in doubt, Orrin, keep your mouth shut."

Though the sky was still a deep dark blue, at twilight, somewhere between night and dawn, I already could tell that this was going to be our best October day yet. Not as cool as the previous mornings, with only a dusting of frost, it reminded me of that faded dog-eared October morning long long ago, when most of me was still new, and everyone that I had ever loved was still alive.

Once at my office, I began to work on the *Oakalla Reporter* with the fervent hope that I would not be interrupted until at least noon. Clarkie called me two hours later.

"That's fast work," I said.

"I figured you were in a hurry, so I stopped by the university on the way to work. You were right. James Garmone's will was there in the archives."

"And?" I said. Since my morning was now shot, I was anxious for the payoff.

"And I can't make anything of it, but maybe you can. It says, and I quote, 'In the event of my death, I leave to the University of Wisconsin all of my worldly possessions, including my home on Lake Mendota, my cabin on Crane Lake, Minnesota, and my eighty acres of old-growth woods on Pine Creek in Adams County, which I would like them to keep in perpetuity as a nature preserve.'"

"That's it, Clarkie!" I said, excited by the news. "You hit the jackpot."

"Do you mind telling me why? No one here at the station could figure it out either."

In the night, I had remembered the huge tree stump on which Abby and I had stood on the bluff there above Pine Creek. If I were to search James Garmone's woods, I bet I would find a lot of those old stumps still around.

"The key words are *old growth,* Clarkie. It's not an old-growth woods now. I'd say most of the trees in it aren't much over thirty years old."

While Clarkie digested that, I glanced outside. Bright blue and still serene, the day was turning out every bit as beautiful as I thought it would be.

"Are you saying that somebody stole James Garmone's trees?"

"Unless there's some record that the university sold them? And I don't think there will be because that would violate his will."

"No. I checked in the archives while I was there. They

sold his house and his cabin and established a scholarship in his name. But that's all they sold."

"Thanks, Clarkie. I owe you one."

"That's a first, isn't it?" For Clarkie, he almost sounded happy. So I didn't remind him that it wasn't a first—not by a long shot.

I tried but could go no further with the *Oakalla Reporter* that morning. Pete Nelson and Milo Thomas were too much on my mind.

After a stop at their homes and then the Corner Bar and Grill, I found them loafing in the Marathon along with Dub Bennett and Sniffy Smith. Dub saw me coming and left by the overhead door as I came in the front door. Dub and I had had an extended session about a year ago, and he still wasn't ready to forgive me for what I had put him through. Sniffy sat on his long-legged stool that serves as his throne, where he could simultaneously talk to people and keep an eye on the drive. Pete and Milo sat on overturned five-gallon cans that someone had dragged in from the back bay years ago.

"Morning, Garth," Sniffy said. "If you're here to pick up Jessie, she's out back. Fit as a fiddle, Danny says."

That'll be the day, I thought. "Where is Danny by the way?" I said. If push came to shove, I might need his help.

"He had to make a wrecker run out on Madison Road. He should be back any time now."

"You'll have to be my witness, then," I said to Sniffy. "I'm arresting Pete and Milo for breaking and entering."

Sniffy gave a loud sniff and nearly fell off his perch. Milo and Pete exchanged glances but said nothing.

"Breaking and entering where?" Sniffy asked.

"Yeah, breaking and entering where?" Milo said. "And if you're wrong about this, badge or no badge, I'm going to have your hide."

"Sniffy, call Sheriff Roberts," I said. "He should hear this, too."

"Sniffy, stay where you are!" Milo said, as Sniffy's head swung back and forth like a gate. "At least we can hear the man out."

"Yeah, we can do that much," Pete said, trying to be peacemaker.

I glanced from Pete to Milo, seeing nothing in either of them that I could hate or even work up a good rage about. If they were in a league with the devil, it didn't show on the outside. But then what was a devil's disciple supposed to look like?

"I'm talking about the *Oakalla Reporter.* You broke in there Sunday and went through my files."

"We didn't break in there," Pete said before Milo could stop him. "The door was already open."

"Pete, goddamn it," Milo said.

"Well, it was. I'm not going to let him pin that on us."

"Open? Or unlocked?" I said.

"Open. Wide, barn-door open," Milo said. "So Pete's right. You can't pin anything on us."

"Breaking and entering doesn't mean you have to break and then enter. Your being there without permission is enough to qualify."

"So sue us," Milo said, starting to rise. "Let's go, Pete."

But Pete showed the character that I never thought I'd see in him. "No, Milo, we ain't leaving here until we hear *all* of what Garth has to say. For thirty years, I've been looking over my shoulder for someone to come along, and now he has. I'm not looking a minute more."

"But, Pete. . ." Milo protested.

"I said *sit!*" Pete slammed his fist down on the five-gallon can beside him. Milo sat back down. "Go on, Garth," Pete said. "Finish what you came to say."

I glanced over at Sniffy who was staring at Pete with wide-eyed admiration. Nothing was ever set in stone, I decided.

"The reason that you came into my building was that you wanted to see what *Freedom's Voice* had to say about the events of 1962, in particular James Garmone's death. Finding nothing to incriminate you, you then came up to Doc Airhart's house. . ."

"Hold it right there, Garth," Pete interrupted. "We didn't go within a block of Doc's place that day, did we, Milo?"

Milo gave Pete a sour look. He reminded me of a ventriloquist who had been upstaged by his dummy. "You're the one doing the talking. If it was up to me, we'd be long gone from here."

"And if it was up to me, we wouldn't be in this mess in the first place. I told you thirty years ago no good would come of it."

"No *good!* No *good!*" Milo exploded. "You might want to throw away the past thirty years, but I don't. Think of where we were before we bought that bull and where we'd be now if we hadn't. He saved our ass, and our future, that's what he did. And you know it, you skinny old fool."

Pete knew it. He could also hear the affection in Milo's voice, along with the anger.

"You're right, Milo," Pete said. "We weren't going much of anywhere before then."

"Then what are we still doing here?"

"Hearing the man out, like I said we would. Go on, Garth. But leave that business about Doc Airhart's be. We were never there."

"Someone was."

Pete's and Milo's shared glance said that they might know who that someone was. "Be that as it may. It wasn't us."

Already I'd lost most of my momentum. When I came into the Marathon, I thought that I had Pete and Milo exactly where I wanted them. Now I wasn't sure that I had them at all.

"Let's go back to James Garmone, his old-growth woods, and the timber that you cut and sold off of it to buy your prize bull. Or are you going to say that didn't happen either?" I said.

Pete checked with Milo first, and when Milo grudgingly nodded his head, Pete said, "It happened. I'm not proud of it. But it happened."

"I *am* proud of it," Milo said. "Best goddamned move I ever made in my life. Why shouldn't I be proud of it?"

"You stole another man's birthright," I said, angry, and not for the first time lately. "And from who knows how many generations the opportunity to walk through an old-growth woods—the only one that I know of in Adams County, and maybe in the whole state."

"Shit, Garth, be reasonable," Milo said, running his hand over his bald head. "How many people knew that it was an old-growth woods? How many people know that today? If so, where the hell are they? I'd think they'd be beating a path to my door right now."

I couldn't deny the truth of what he said. Had anybody at the University of Wisconsin taken a real interest thirty years ago, something would have happened then.

"Still, Milo, it's the principle of the thing."

"Principle, my ass. You can't eat them, you can't milk them, and you sure as hell can't grow them. We were going under, Garth. What else were we supposed to do? And don't say find something else, because we were no good at that either. Nothing, Garth. We were never good at anything. Until we bought that bull."

"With blood money."

"Whose blood, Garth?"

"James Garmone's."

"James Garmone tripped and fell and drowned in Pine Creek. Read your old newspapers if you don't believe me."

"That's what you hope happened, that's what you want to believe happened, but that's not what happened, and you and I both know it."

I was looking at Milo as I spoke. I didn't think that Pete would have been a partner to murder, no matter what he stood to gain from it.

"Say it's not true, Milo," Pete said.

"It's not true, Pete. Garth here is confusing facts with fiction. I never killed anybody and don't know anyone who has."

"But you suspect somebody, don't you, Milo?" I said.

"He was there in the neighborhood that day. That's all I'll say."

"Who, Milo?" Pete asked.

Milo stood, then used his foot to shove his can out of the way. He planned to leave, and nobody there was going to stop him.

"Garth knows who," he said. "That's all I have to say on the subject. You coming, Pete?"

Pete couldn't get off of his can fast enough. "Coming, Milo."

Sniffy and I watched them leave. He had forgotten all about the drive that he was supposed to be watching for Danny.

"What do you think, Sniffy? Are they telling the truth?"

He came out with a couple short, sharp sniffs while he thought about it. Sniffy liked to be included, even if up until then, he'd had no opinion on the subject.

"I believe they are, Garth. Much to my surprise."

"What's to your surprise, Pete and Milo, or the fact that you believe them?"

"The fact that I believe them, anybody for that matter. Sometimes I feel like that guy with the lamp out looking for an honest man."

"Diogenes."

"What's that, Garth?"

Sniffy's eyes were on the drive where someone had just pulled in for gas. Sniffy hated to pump gas, so he always tried to outwait whoever pulled in, hoping that they would pull back out again.

"Diogenes. That was the man with the lantern's name."

"Crap," Sniffy said as he bailed off the stool and hurried to the door on his way to the drive. "Here comes Danny."

On my way out, I took Jessie's key off the peg beside the door. Though I didn't know what for, I might need her later.

CHAPTER 22

I stopped by home to check with Ruth before I made my way to the west end of town. No, she hadn't seen Shank Doyles' name on the list of mourners at Doc's funeral, but she could double-check it for me if I wanted. I said not to bother, that I doubted if it would be there.

Then I asked her if she had yet found anyone who lived in the orphanage in 1962. She said that she was following a couple leads and might have something for me by noon. By noon, I said, if I survived until then, I hoped to have this thing wrapped up.

"Be careful" were her parting words to me.

Shank Doyle wasn't in his office but down in the mill amidst the saws, belts, and dust, the whir of men and logs, that I found confusing and more than a little threatening.

Shank was overseeing the sawing of a huge pine log, the smell alone of whose resin made me feel lightheaded and unsure of my footing. My brain kept saying to run while I had the chance. But mesmerized by all of the machinery, and Shank's seemingly effortless control of it, I stayed. Right up until the time that the noon whistle blew.

"What is it now, Ryland?" Shank said as the mill shut down and the men cleared out. "And it better be good."

Shank wore goggles, jeans, steel-toed work boots, and a green flannel shirt that was caked with sawdust. But unlike every one of his men, he wore no hard hat or chaps.

"I thought we might talk in your office."

"This is my office," he said as he took off his goggles and let them hang by their elastic strap around his neck. "That up there is where I go to hide."

I looked around the mill where not a soul was in sight. They had emptied the mill faster than rats from a sinking ship.

"I guess this will have to do, then," I said.

We stood on a catwalk overlooking the mill's main saw, a vicious-looking monster that Shank affectionately called the "Great White." I didn't know the "Great White's" rating, but it had made short work of the pine. Glancing outside, out of the dark into the light, I longed to feel the sun upon my face.

"Speak, Ryland. I don't have all day."

Shank dusted himself off then rolled up his sleeves. His forearms, I noted, appeared to be all bone.

"I just had a talk with Pete and Milo," I said. "They told me where they got the money to buy their prize bull."

Shank Doyle wasn't impressed. "So what does that make me, their pimp?"

"Of sorts. They stole James Garmone's woods, and you sold it for them. Or you helped them steal it. Either way, it amounts to the same thing."

Shank's eyes were on the "Great White." They saw something that I didn't see. He started down the catwalk toward it. I followed him.

"Even if that were true, Ryland, the statute of limitations ran out on that a long time ago, so you've got yourself all in a lather over nothing."

Shank went over to examine the saw blade. I stopped well short of it.

"Not for the IRS, it hasn't. Not if your intent was to defraud or deceive," I said.

Satisfied that the blade was still in working order, Shank then began to check out the conveyor belt that delivered the logs. "You'd put me through all of that for just a few trees?" There was clear menace in his voice.

"Not just a few trees, Shank. Eighty acres of old-growth forest. Most of it black walnut, by my estimate."

He turned his eyes on me. They had a chilling lack of conscience in them. "Supposing you're right, black walnut was only worth a fraction then what it is now. The overseas market hadn't even got going good yet. It might as well have been poplar that we stole."

I didn't buy that and neither did Shank. He was just testing the water.

"Whatever you got for them, they were worth a sawmill and a prize bull. Even if you sold them here, which I doubt."

"What would be the profit in that?" he said, starting my way. "You can't make any money buying timber for somebody else."

As he came toward me, I retreated a couple steps back up the catwalk. Not knowing what he had in mind, I didn't want to be like Eugene and wait until he was within arm's reach to find out.

"Are you afraid of me, Ryland? If not, you should be."

His balled fists said that he wasn't kidding. I kept backpedaling as he kept coming.

"Sure, I'm afraid of you, Shank. I'd be a fool not to be. But by the same token, you ought to be afraid of me."

That stopped him in his tracks. He couldn't laugh and walk at the same time.

"You've got balls, Ryland, I'll give you that. The balls of a flea crawling up an elephant's leg yelling rape."

We stared at each other for what to me seemed longer than it was. Then he abruptly turned away to rest his hands on the railing of the catwalk. All around him, he could see his life's work, which at that moment was to my advantage. It seemed the only thing in life Shank Doyle really cared about, and he wasn't willing to risk losing it over me.

"So what will it take, Ryland, short of killing you, to get you out of my hair for good?"

"The truth about James Garmone."

"That's easy enough. A couple of kids drowned him."

I was too shocked by that revelation to say anything.

Shank went on. "I was on my way to see Milo Thomas about some timber that he wanted to sell me, when crossing Wildwood Bridge I saw what looked like a couple kids running up the bank and into the woods. So I stopped to see what they were running from, and that's when I saw the professor's body floating in the creek. Though I didn't know it was him until I got down to the creek. He was dead. Near as I could tell anyway. So I dragged him off to one side and left him there, figuring it was none of my business."

"Which side of the creek did you leave him on?" I said.

"The west side. The side I came down on."

Which was the shallow side and opposite of where

James Garmone had been found.

"Why did you figure it was none of your business?" I said.

Shank turned my way. If he felt any remorse or regret, I didn't see it on his face.

"The man was an asshole, Ryland. He practically threw me out of his office when I asked about buying some of those trees of his. Said he'd rot in hell before he'd let even one of them be cut. And that was after I'd spent half a day chasing him down in Madison."

"The price of doing business," I said.

"They were *trees*, for Christ sake!" he said as his face contorted and his hands once again became fists. "It's not like I was asking for one of his kids or anything."

I let that pass. There was no use debating the value of a tree, any tree, with someone who cut them for a living. It was like debating the value of a gun with a cop. It all depended on your perspective—on who owned the tree and who held the gun.

"How did you know the trees were there?" I said.

"I found them one day when I was coon hunting. My old Nig treed in there, and when I started shinning the tree, I forgot all about the coon in it. Almost all the other trees in there were the same way—three to four feet across and at least thirty feet to the first limb." Shank's eyes were shining now. "Damndest woods I ever saw. To tell you the truth, Ryland, from that day forward, I started thinking of it as *my* woods."

"So it wasn't exactly none of your business if James Garmone died," I said. "I'd say it meant a lot to your business."

"Since then, yes. At the time, no."

"Then when did you start having second thoughts about James Garmone and his woods?"

Shank glanced at his Timex as some of his workers

started to filter back into the mill. But either out of fear, or respect, they kept their distance.

"When I drove up the road to talk to Milo. He took me back to show me his woods, and there probably weren't more than a half-dozen trees worth cutting in it, and I told him so. How about Pete's woods, he said? The same thing. Most of the good timber had been sold out of them before they ever bought their farms. What were he and Pete going to do, he said? They needed a bull for their herds and a dozen-odd trees weren't going to buy them one. So I said to give me a week or two and maybe I could work something out. That's when I lined up a buyer for the professor's trees."

"Before he was even cold yet."

Shank took offense. "He was cold when I found him, Ryland. Don't try to make me feel guilty because I don't. He didn't need that woods anymore, but I did."

"And what was your split with Pete and Milo, a third all the way around?"

"Half and half. They got half, and I got half. After all, I was doing all the work, taking all the risk. All they were doing was providing a cover for me. I sold their trees here at the sawmill to cover my butt on that, and I sold my trees to the buyer I found in Madison. It took me nearly all summer, working seven days a week, but I got the job done."

Shank was proud of himself. In my own way, I was proud of him, too. I didn't like what he had done, but I liked the guts it took to do it. And the iron-man will to see it through.

"I'd like to go back to the beginning," I said.

He glanced at his watch again. "You've got five minutes. Then you're out of here."

"You say you saw a couple boys running away as you drove up to the bridge. Which way were they going?"

"East."

"Did you recognize either one of them?"

"No. I only caught a glimpse of them."

"Then how can you say that one of them was Dewey Clinton?" In our first meeting, Shank had said as much.

"What good will it do to know that now?" he said. Shank's look said that he didn't want to tell me.

"Maybe none. Maybe a whole lot. It depends on what your answer is."

With a shrug of his shoulders, Shank decided in my favor. "I can't say that I saw Dewey then. But, when I came back through the bridge about an hour later, the professor's body was back in the water, and Dewey was walking up the road toward home. What's the matter, Dewey? I said as I pulled up alongside him. You look like you lost your last friend. 'Have,' he said with tears in his eyes. 'Have lost my last friend.' Then he got this wild look in his eyes and took off running for home."

The one o'clock whistle sounded. But Shank and I both ignored it.

"Do you really think Dewey killed James Garmone?" I said.

"I think he played a part in it. If not so then, I do now."

"Why now?"

"Think about it, Ryland. Why else would Dewey hang himself?"

"For killing Eugene Yuill."

Shank's laugh said that wasn't even a possibility. "You know better, Ryland. If you don't, I do."

I wondered what else Shank knew that he wasn't telling me. But for now I'd concentrate on James Garmone.

"Could the two boys that you saw have been from the orphanage?"

"They could have been. They could have been from the moon, too. I don't know who they were or where they were from."

Looking out over the mill, I noticed how quiet it was in there. No one seemed willing to push a button without Shank's say so. I guessed that kind of power was both good and bad. Nothing got broken, but nothing got done either when you weren't around.

"And you never heard about anyone finding another body in the creek there below the bridge?"

Shank hesitated before he answered. He was about done with me now, he thought. He didn't want to say any more than he had to.

"I saw the sheriff's car and Doc Airhart's car parked there beside the bridge a week or so after that. But I dismissed it at the time because I figured they were still trying to get a handle on what happened to James Garmone, since the account in the paper was no way close to right, and they had to know that."

"How long did you go on believing that all they were doing there was investigating James Garmone's death?"

"Until that night at the Corner Bar and Grill when Dewey started spouting off about finding two bodies."

"That's when you put two and two together and came up with what? Dewey?" I said.

"Who else, Garth? If there was a second killing, who else in Oakalla besides Dewey could have done it?"

"You could have."

"But I didn't."

There was no way to read him, to see through those cold off-green eyes of his. Even if he had killed James Garmone and the boy whose bones were in Doc's morgue, it wouldn't have shown up on his face.

"And you still say Dewey couldn't have killed

Eugene," I said. "That doesn't make sense to me."

"It doesn't have to make sense to you. Just to me."

I was dismissed. With a wave of his hand that set his men in motion, Shank Doyle went back to work.

Ruth had lunch waiting for me when I got home. Even if it was leftover chili I was glad, because I didn't feel like going to the Corner Bar and Grill to eat.

"What's wrong?" she asked as I sat down at the table.

"I'm at a dead end again. Either Shank Doyle lied to me or he told me the truth. I don't know which. Even if I did know, I don't know what I'd do with it. We have any peanut butter?" I'd searched the table without seeing any.

"What do you want peanut butter for?" she asked as she reached into the cabinet for it.

"And celery. Blame it on too many school lunches as a kid. We always had peanut butter and celery, though not always one on top the other, with our chili."

She rummaged through the refrigerator before she found the celery. "Anything else before I sit down?"

"Answers, Ruth. I need a whole bushel basket of them."

"Sorry, Garth. You came to the wrong place."

She sat down at the table, and we began to eat. As we did, I told her what I'd learned from Shank Doyle.

"It sounds like he's telling the truth to me," she said. "Otherwise, why bring up the other boys at all? Why not just blame it all on Dewey?"

"We don't know that one of the *other* boys wasn't Dewey."

"We don't know it was either."

"There's a difference, Ruth," I said as I chewed on a stalk of celery laden with peanut butter. "Two boys and it all comes down to Dewey. Three boys and the possibilities are endless."

"How do you figure?"

I blew on my chili and then shoveled a spoonful into

my mouth. Like a lot of things that come to mind, it was better the second time around.

"Let's say that for whatever the reason, Dewey makes friends with a boy from the orphanage. Let's further say that for whatever the reason, this boy talks Dewey into dropping a rock on James Garmone's head. Maybe it's one of those spur of the moment things. You know, like kids do. And maybe he doesn't really think that Dewey will do it. But to his surprise, and maybe even to his delight, Dewey does do it. Hits James Garmone over the head and cold-cocks him right there in the middle of Pine Creek. Kills him, as it turns out, since by the time the boys get down there and find him, he's drowned. Then they hear Shank coming, panic, and run off into the woods. Later though, when they return, they find James Garmone on shore where Shank has lain him, and where no one is going to believe that he fell, hit his head, and drowned. So they drag him back into the water."

"I'm with you so far." Ruth was chewing on a stalk of celery, sans peanut butter, which she probably wouldn't have eaten had she been starving because she ate so much of it during the Depression.

"As a result, however, Dewey's friend, who is an orphan and who doesn't need any bad press, tells Dewey that he's trouble and wants nothing more to do with him."

I saw Ruth's eyes light up, which meant that she knew something I didn't. But I would have to wait.

"So Dewey goes into a funk, tries to win his friend back, and ends up killing him."

"How?" Ruth was skeptical.

"Maybe they camped out together, and Dewey put a pillow over his head. How do I know, Ruth? But that would certainly explain why Dewey kept insisting that 'He done it.' "

"Killing James Garmone would be enough to explain

that," she said. When I couldn't muster an argument for that, she continued, "And it also leaves a lot of other things unexplained, like who killed Doc Airhart and Eugene Yuill and why? Unless you're planning on pinning those murders on Dewey, too?"

"Maybe somebody killed them for a completely different reason, and Dewey got caught in the cross fire. I know Dewey didn't need any help throwing that rock at me."

"You're sure it was Dewey?" She still had her doubts about that.

"Absolutely, Ruth. Howdy Heavin's sure, too. He was with Dewey at the time, remember?"

Ruth absentmindedly stirred her chili, which meant that she was locked in a thought. "Let's go on to the three boys."

"Same setting, except now it's a trio. Dewey takes the fall, and the two boys, let's say they're both from the orphanage, split. What do they owe him anyway? He's just a big dumb cluck they used to entertain themselves. And the friend that Dewey thinks he's lost is James Garmone, who has taken Dewey under his wing in his travels up and down Pine Creek."

"That leaves us up the same tree, Garth. Who killed Doc and Eugene and why? Also, none of it explains how the boy who died ended up in Pine Creek, if in fact he did. Even if Dewey did kill him, he wasn't smart enough to leave him in the creek, and then go tell the world that he 'done it.'"

She had me there. Neither one of my scenarios made complete sense all the way through. But I wasn't ready to give up.

"Doc was probably protecting Dewey. I'm certain of that," I said. "Otherwise, he never would have let that story about James Garmone's accidental drowning stand, or, with the help of the sheriff, covered up the second death."

"Then why didn't he and the sheriff pursue either death? I know enough about Doc and Maynard Lutes both that they wouldn't have let two murders stand, even if Dewey had done them."

"I don't know, Ruth. Do you?" Her cat-that-ate-the-canary look said she might.

"Maybe. Does the name Adelle Holland mean anything to you?"

"No. Should it?"

"I thought it might. She's the one who used to run the orphanage. The word I get is that she didn't much care how she did it either."

My chili was getting cold. I tried to eat faster. "Go on. You have my undivided attention."

"Wipe your chin," she said.

I did as she asked.

Ruth continued, "What I mean by that is that the welfare of the children was her least concern. Her greatest concern was what she could get for one of them, so once a child got to be around twelve or so, or proved to be a troublemaker, she saw to it that they soon got their walking papers."

"Let me get this straight. Are you saying that she sold the kids? And those that she couldn't sell, she made hit the road?"

"In a nutshell, yes. There might have been exceptions, where she went through all of the proper channels, but for the most part, she loaded and unloaded them as fast as she could. A few even ended up here in Oakalla, but none stayed that I know of."

"That you know of."

"I'm working on that, Garth. One thing at a time."

"Go ahead. I'm sorry for the interruption."

"There's not much more to say. But if there was trouble concerning any of the children in the orphanage, Adelle Holland would have done her best to hide it, because the last thing that she would have wanted was an investigation of her orphanage."

"To the point of murder?"

I expected Ruth to deny it. She didn't. "All that I've learned about the woman says that she was capable of about anything. So I wouldn't rule out murder at this point."

"But the orphanage closed twenty years ago. She could be dead now."

"Not dead, Garth. Alive and well and living in White Lake."

White Lake was the only town of any size east of Oakalla until you got to Oshkosh. A town of about fifteen thousand, it had the reputation for having a lot of hundred-dollar millionaires.

"You don't by chance have her address, do you?"

I was rewarded with one of Ruth's rare smiles. "By chance, I do."

CHAPTER 23

I was on my way to the back door when Abby came in the front door. Surprised at seeing her in the middle of the day, it took me a moment to realize that she was living there now. I waited for her in the kitchen.

"You had lunch?" I said.

"Yes. I ate at the hospital."

"Good. Then you can come with me to White Lake."

She took about two seconds to say, "Why don't you come with me to White Lake?"

"You don't want to ride in Jessie?"

"Not if I can help it."

"You've been talking to Ruth, I see."

Like the morning, her smile had a touch of frost to it. "I can make up my own mind about some things, Garth."

We were ten miles out of town before we spoke again. I entertained myself by looking out the window—at alfalfa and winter wheat, both still green and growing; barns, cows, sky, and trees; pumpkins piled in wagons alongside the road, houses with homesteads, former homesteads without houses, cornfields, windmills, and gardens gone to seed; crossroads where towns used to be; and occasionally looking over at Abby—at her blue-green eyes and yellow hair. Sometimes I still found it hard to believe, when I saw her at my side, that she was there.

"Is this the right time?" she finally said.

"To do what?"

"Talk about Diana."

"I told you. There's nothing to talk about."

"Were you involved with her?"

"Yes," trying to keep my voice neutral.

"Then there's something to talk about."

I groaned. Apparently she had never heard my grandfather's advice to my father.

"What do you want to know about Diana? Did I love her? Yes. Do I still love her? I don't know. As a friend maybe, but most friends stay in touch, and we don't. Did I love her as much as I do you? Don't expect me to answer that question because I'm not the same person now as I was then. But since you're asking, and if you're not, I love you better than I loved her. For all of the right reasons and none of the wrong ones."

"Even if I didn't have this car?"

"Even if you drove an Edsel. She had a Bentley, by the way."

"Oh? She was rich, then. Was she a doctor, like me?"

"No. She was married to one."

"It's still nice that you could keep it in the family. Professionally speaking, of course. Did Ruth ever let her spend the night with you, or did you spend your nights with her?"

I didn't know how far we had gone since this conversation started, but I hadn't once looked at the road. We could be on a ferry to Muskegon for all I knew.

"If you're jealous, don't be," I said. "Ruth would barely let Diana in the house and then leave the room whenever she was there."

"Why? Were her instincts better than yours?"

I thought it over and decided that I couldn't tell her the whole story without more explanation than I cared to go into. "Ruth would have liked Diana fine, if she had thought Diana was doing right by me."

It was the wrong thing to say, but then, under the circumstances, there wasn't a right thing to say.

"So, I'm about to go on Ruth's shit list, is that it?" She was on the verge of tears.

"By leaving Oakalla, you mean?"

"Yes. By leaving. What else would I mean?"

"You'll have to talk to Ruth about that. She keeps her own counsel in all such matters."

Silent again for a long stretch of road, she then said, "It was a mistake, Garth."

I felt a sudden tightness in my chest that had nothing to do with the rows of pines that crowded the road on either side. "What was a mistake? Us?"

"No. Not us. Never us. Staying at your house was a mistake. I thought it could never work, not even for a day, and it has. I like it there. Too much, I'm afraid, for my own good. I feel safe there."

"Isn't that what home is supposed to feel like?"

"Exactly."

Then I saw what she was getting at. "But it's not home?"

"No. Not yet anyway. Maybe not ever. Leaving was

going to be hard enough. Now it's going to be that much harder."

"Then don't leave." It seemed the perfect solution to me.

"Then I'll always wonder if I did the right thing."

"You're going to wonder anyway, regardless."

She shook her head no. "I'll never wonder about us, Garth. There in Oakalla, we would live happily forever after. I'm sure of that now. But that's not what I want. . ."

"You want to live unhappily forever after?"

"Let me finish. For now. That's not what I want for now. What I want to do is learn to be the best pathologist I can be. Then I can decide what in the end matters the most to me."

"Once you leave, you won't come back," I said.

"You don't know that, Garth. Neither do I. Give us that much, at least."

I did know that, but there was no use arguing the point. The instant your heart hit the road, it started burning its bridges behind it. Not as a matter of choice, perhaps, but of survival.

"Okay, I'll give us that," I said.

"Say it like you mean it."

I tried, but nothing would come out.

Adelle Holland lived in White Lake's high-rent district between the White Lake Country Club and White Lake itself. Her yard alone was worth millions—five acres of bluegrass and blue spruce in the form of a small peninsula that gently sloped down to the water with a small cozy bay on one side of it and a long, wide sweep of lake on the other. Her house was white brick with a red roof and three red brick chimneys. A six-foot-high black wrought-iron fence ran on either side of her red brick driveway all the way to, and including, the circle drive in front of her house. Century-old pines shaded the house and left their cones along the drive. A thick brown carpet of pine needles crunched underfoot as Abby and I made our way through the pines and out into the sunlight, where a tall, white-haired woman, wearing canvas shoes, gray slacks, a pink windbreaker, and sunglasses, stared out into the lake.

"Adelle Holland?" I said.

Though the woman at first appeared to be alone, I saw that she had a companion nearby. A large coarse-featured man about her age with thin black hair and thick black brows knelt on the ground and appeared to be cutting flowers for a bouquet. His ponderous movements made me wonder what was the matter with him, if he were drugged or perhaps had suffered a stroke recently.

"Yes. I'm Adelle Holland."

The woman who turned to face me was neither as old nor as frail as I had expected her to be. Somewhere in her sixties (by my guess), she had a Roman nose to go with her straight white hair and fair skin, thin lips, and strong chin, and a handsome, if not arresting face. She fit Ruth's description of someone who knew what she wanted and how to get it.

"Who are you?" she said, obviously not much interested.

"I'm Garth Ryland. I own and edit the *Oakalla Reporter.* This is Dr. Abby Airhart. She is the surgeon at the Adams County Hospital."

I could tell by the tilt of Adelle Holland's nose that with that introduction, we rose a little in her estimation. Not quite as high as senator or governor, but above Jehovah's Witness.

"Dr. Airhart?" she said with interest. "Any relation to *the* Dr. Airhart?"

"I'm. . ." Abby's face fell. ". . . *was* his niece. Uncle Bill died a week ago today."

"I'm sorry to hear that. I knew your Uncle Bill. He was

a fine man."

I studied her as she spoke. Her voice had a slight quaver to it, as if she, too, had some sort of affliction. I wished I could see her eyes. Then I would better know who she was.

We three stood there a moment without saying anything further, as the man nearby, with flowers in one hand and scissors in the other, rose unsteadily and went in search of more flowers. I saw that he walked with a noticeable limp.

"My husband," Adelle Holland said, her eyes on him every step of the way as if to help guide his path. "He was in a terrible accident a few years ago. He hasn't been the same since."

Common-law husband, my instinct said. "The reason we're here, Mrs. Holland. . ."

"*Miss* Holland," she corrected, without offering an explanation. My instinct, it appeared, was right.

"The reason we're here, Miss Holland, is that we're investigating what might have been a murder in the early 1960s, when you were still in charge of the orphanage there north of Oakalla."

At the word orphanage, her face assumed the same sour look that mine used to at the mention of cod-liver oil. "I believe they are called children's homes now. That's what I would prefer mine to be called."

Seeing that she was going to be a third party to this discussion, Abby went after the man with the limp. She caught up to him as he bent over another flower bed out near the water.

"Cecil and his flowers," Adelle Holland said, with tenderness it seemed. "What would he ever do without them?"

For a moment, we watched Abby and Cecil, as she held his bouquet for him, then took each flower as he cut it.

"You have a good one there," Adelle Holland said as

she turned back to me.

"Are we that obvious?" Because I didn't think we were.

"If one knows what to look for. I do."

She started walking slowly toward the lake, but away from where Abby and Cecil were. I went with her.

"You have a beautiful place," I said as we walked. "It must be worth a mint."

"It is," she said. "And everybody and his brother wants it. The town of White Lake, the country club, the White Sails Yacht Club. If you're planning on buying it, you'll have to get in line." The quaver in her voice, I noted, got better as we went along. Maybe the walking helped, made her less conscious of it.

"I can't afford it," I said.

"Neither can I. But I plan to hang on to it to my last breath. Then what do I care who fights over the remains."

"What about Cecil?"

"Oh, I'll outlive him," she said with certainty. "If only because he couldn't survive without me."

Ruth was right. Adelle Holland was one tough cookie. But in spite of myself, I found that I liked her.

"You said something about a murder, in the early 1960s. Could you be more specific?" she said.

"Nineteen sixty-two, to be exact. James Garmone, who was a zoology professor at the University of Wisconsin, was found drowned under Wildwood Bridge. Do you remember the incident?"

"I remember. I thought it was an accidental drowning."

"I have reason to believe otherwise."

We stood at the water's edge with the waves lapping at our feet. To our right, in the small bay, a pair of mallards were weaving in and out of the lily pads. Surrounded with the lake smell I loved, I wanted to stand there forever, just drinking it in.

"Forgive me for asking, Mr. Ryland, but what has James Garmone's death to do with me?"

"There's more to the story."

"There usually is."

"I also have reason to believe that one of the boys from your orphanage was murdered shortly thereafter."

Purposely I omitted the details, hoping that she might fill me in. I should have known better. Adelle Holland didn't acquire this piece of paradise by being either soft—or dumb.

"May I hear your reasons why you think one of my boys was murdered?" The tremor in her voice had returned. I wished that I could see into her eyes.

"His body turned up, after all of these years."

"Where was it being kept?"

"A whiskey barrel in Doc Airhart's morgue."

"I see," she said. And, if I judged by the sound of her voice, she did see, much more than I did.

"It's true, then," she said. "I thought Dr. Airhart was being overly dramatic when he called it murder, that Buddy had simply run away and drowned."

"Buddy?"

"Buddy Brewer, the boy in question."

"He didn't drown. I can testify to that."

Adelle Holland sat down in the grass. I sat down beside her. We looked out across the lake, which on this Wednesday in October, had one lone fishing boat on it, anchored along the point at the mouth of the bay.

"Doc Airhart *did* question you about him, then?" I said.

For the first time since our arrival, Adelle Holland took off her sunglasses—briefly to wipe something from them before putting them back on again. Her eyes, I noticed, were blue and watery. Sentiment? The parade of ghosts marching through her memory? Or just the breeze off the lake?

"Did Dr. Airhart say that he did?" she asked.

"You did. I never got the chance to ask him."

"Is there something that you need to tell me about Dr. Airhart, Mr. Ryland?" She apparently thought there was.

"He was murdered in his sleep. Someone held a pillow over his face."

She shuddered, looked away. "Poor Buddy," she said.

"I was talking about Doc Airhart."

"I know."

While I worked my way through that, she kept her gaze on the lake. I could tell by her pallor that I had awakened in her a secret horror.

She said, "Dr. Airhart did come to me asking about Buddy. I said we had no child there who matched that description. He must have come from somewhere else."

"You didn't want trouble, is that it, anyone looking too closely at the orphanage?"

"Children's home," she corrected.

"What kind of home is it when you sell the children?"

"A profitable one," she said. Her arm swept the shoreline. "As you can see."

"Then you don't deny it?"

"What's to deny? People wanted children. I provided them with children. I was a matchmaker. I found homes for hundreds of children who otherwise would never have had a home of their own."

"And booted out those who either were too old to adopt or somehow didn't fit your bill."

"With good reason," she said, rising to her feet. "The one time I didn't do that, listened to my foolish heart, instead of my head, it cost me."

I rose to confront her. "Cost you what?" My arm followed the same arc that hers had taken. "Another foot of shoreline?"

"Buddy."

"What?" I said, not sure I heard her right.

"It cost me Buddy, my favorite child of all."

She had started walking back toward the house. All I could do was walk with her.

"Are you going to explain that to me or leave me out on my limb?" I said.

"There is nothing to explain. I made a mistake in judgment, and it cost Buddy his life."

"What mistake in judgment?"

I stopped. The closer to the house we came, the worse her quaver became. I was afraid that once we reached our starting point, she wouldn't be able to speak at all. I wondered why until I saw that the house's deep all-consuming shadow more than matched that of the orphanage.

"A boy," she said in answer to my question. "A terrible wicked boy with the smile of an angel and the soul of the devil. I knew he was trouble from the moment he appeared on my doorstep, but like the serpent he was, he deceived me into taking him in."

"Describe him to me. Perhaps I know him."

She tried. I could see her strain under the effort. But it was in vain.

"I can't. When he left, I put him out of my mind for good, for fear he might return at my most unguarded moment, and that's where he has stayed."

"Where did he go, and what was his name?"

"His name was Roger. Roger Farmer, or at least that's what his papers said. As for where he went, I can't tell you."

"Can't or won't?"

"Can't. One day, without even calling me first, a couple came by the children's home, looking for a son. I told them I didn't operate that way. One had to go through the proper channels. . ." She stopped to explain. "I had to be careful, you understand. There were those in the social services who would have shut me down if they could have."

With good reason, I thought.

"But the couple were quite insistent, especially the woman, so I lined all the boys up, and without even a moment's hesitation, she chose Roger." Even yet, Adelle Holland felt the power of that moment. "Thank God! I cried in silent prayer. The curse has been lifted!"

"You feared Roger Farmer that much?"

"I feared him with my *life.* So did the children, except for Buddy who worshiped him."

My thoughts were racing ahead of me. Like Adelle Holland, I found it hard to keep the quaver out of my voice. "Did the couple take Roger home with them that same day?" If so, I was at another dead end.

She shook her head. "No. They had not brought any money, and I was, if nothing else, greedy in those days. Today I would have given him to them."

"Hindsight is always twenty-twenty." Except mine, which was twenty-fifty.

She started walking again. "To conclude the matter, Mr. Ryland. By the time they returned with the money, Buddy was dead."

"Was this before or after James Garmone's death?"

"After. Shortly after. Which led me to wonder if Buddy may have played a part in it?"

She was asking as much as musing, but I didn't have an answer for her. "I thought you said Buddy was your favorite?"

"I said Buddy was my favorite. I didn't say Buddy was without fault." We came to the end of the sunlight and plunged into the shadow ahead. "And in Roger Farmer's hands. . . who knows what he may have become?"

"Do you have any idea why Roger Farmer might have

wanted to kill James Garmone, assuming he did?"

We stopped when we came to where Abby and Cecil were standing. "For the pleasure of it, I assume."

Cecil wore a shy smile as he handed Adelle Holland a bouquet of zinnias and mums, then limped off in the direction of the house. Her expression was one of love and pity, as she took off her sunglasses to watch him go. There were still a lot of questions left unanswered, but I no longer felt like asking them.

"Thank you, Miss Holland," I said.

She nodded. We left.

"Well?" Abby said as we pulled out of the driveway.

I told her what I had learned from Adelle Holland.

"Do you think Roger Farmer is somehow in Oakalla?" she said.

"I don't see how he could be, Abby. He would have surfaced long before now."

"You mean he would have killed someone?"

I nodded.

"How do you know he hasn't?"

"I don't. But if he had been in Oakalla from then until now, surely someone would have recognized him for what he was. If not Doc, then Rupert. If not Rupert, then Ruth or I."

"Perhaps Uncle Bill did recognize him. Remember? Maybe that's what got him killed."

"What got him killed were his 1962 memoirs. We don't know that Roger Farmer did it."

"We don't know that he didn't either."

We rode in silence for a while, kept the rush-hour traffic company as some of the working people left White Lake proper for their homes in the outlying subdivisions. All of them seemed in a hurry, but to get to what, I didn't know. Used to know but had forgotten.

Then I said, "What did you learn from Cecil in all of

that time?"

"I learned that he used to be a truck driver, until his accident, that he loves flowers, and. . ." Her smile gave her away. "He thought that I was pretty okay, too."

"That goes without saying. How old is Cecil anyway?"

"Too old to be Roger Farmer."

"It was worth a shot."

Our next silence seemed to drag on and on. I found it hard to voice my thoughts, and Abby appeared to be having the same problem. And the sun, now low in the southwest, was in our eyes the whole time.

"What's bothering you, Garth?" she said. "Besides Roger Farmer?"

"That should be enough, I'd think."

"It should be, but it's not."

I smiled at her. She knew me too well.

"Just thinking about things," I said. "Pete Nelson, Milo Thomas, Shank Doyle, Adelle Holland. The list could go on and on, but I'll stop there. They all broke the rules, they all cheated at life, and they all have prospered because of it. Then there's Eugene Yuill who played by the rules all of his life, who didn't know how to cheat because it wasn't in him, and he gets hit over the head and stuffed into the trunk of his car. Not to mention Dewey Clinton, who really never had much of a shot at life in the first place, but at least tried to do the right thing as far as he saw it. I keep trying to make sense out of it all, but I can't. Life, it seems, should be fairer than that."

She reached over and took my hand. I loved the feel of her. Her touch was life itself.

"Aren't you the one who told me not to expect life to be fair?" she said.

"I am."

"Now you've changed your mind?"

"No. But it doesn't mean I have to like it."

"Or accept it either, if I know you."

Now that I'd started, I might as well tell her all of it. "I'm a dinosaur, Abby, part of a dying breed. I want life to be fair but know it's not, and I want justice to reign but know it won't. Maybe that's why I still believe in God, that He will make all things right in the end."

"The things that you can't, you mean?"

"Yes. He is my avenger, the savior of all goodness, the righter of all wrongs."

She was silent for a moment, then said, "Have you ever thought that perhaps you are His?"

CHAPTER 24

We were stopped in front of my house. I already had one foot out the door, but so far Abby had made no move in that direction.

"Aren't you coming in?" I said.

"No. I've got to make some rounds at the hospital. A couple of my patients aren't doing as well as I'd like, and I've got to try to figure out what we're doing wrong. It will probably be late before I get home." Then she corrected herself. *"Back.* Before I get back here."

"I'll see you then, I hope."

"Why wouldn't you?"

"I've still got a full day's work on the *Oakalla Reporter* that I haven't even started yet." I'd swung my other foot out the door and had both on the ground when the neighbor's cat chose that moment to cross the street for home. "Damn," I said, as I swung both feet back inside the Prelude. "Take me to my office, will you? I forgot to check on the cats."

The first thing that I saw when I walked into my office was Eugene's gun and holster lying on my desk where Ben Bryan had left them. It jolted me to see them there, reminded me of the stakes involved.

What I also saw there on my desk was the beginning of the *Oakalla Reporter,* whose deadline was less than thirty-six hours away. In all of my years as a newspaperman, I hadn't missed a deadline yet. But this might be my first.

Starting in 1962, I went backwards for five years, stopping with the July 12, 1957, issue of *Freedom's Voice,* but found no mention of any dead cats either in Oakalla's south end or anywhere else. Puzzled, I rested my eyes a moment as I tried to think this thing through. For a period of ten years, 1957 to 1967, no cats had been killed in Oakalla on a mass scale by anyone. When then had it started and why had it ended?

The phone rang. It was Ruth. "Try 1968" was all she said before she hung up.

I tried 1968. For a period of six months, January to June, cats had died in Oakalla's south end on a regular basis. Some had been found frozen in the ice, some had been buried under the snow, some had been left lying in the street, others on their masters' front porches. All, or nearly all, appeared to have been strangled. Then in July 1968, the cat killings stopped.

I grabbed Eugene's gun and holster on my way out the door. Between sunset and stars, the sky was so clear it was almost glossy, and someone somewhere, God love him, was burning leaves, as its blue haze took over the town and gave me a taste of falls gone by.

I tried not to run, but the closer I came to home, the faster I walked, until I might as well have been running. And though it wasn't my intention, I nearly scared the stuffing out of both Ruth and Daisy when I burst in the back door.

"What's that for?" Ruth asked, eyeing Eugene's revolver.

"I figured I might need it before the night is through."

"You might at that."

Having recovered from her scare, Daisy still wasn't sure what to make of me. She approached me cautiously, eyes wary, tail at half-mast, the way she used to approach Doc after he had reprimanded her for breaking point.

"Sorry, Daisy," I said, reaching down to scratch her chin. "I was in a hurry."

"Sorry, Daisy? What about Ruth?" she said.

"Sorry, Ruth. But I think that time is of the essence."

"You figure he'll fly the coop?"

"Whoever *he* is, yes. So why don't you enlighten me?"

"Why don't you light first. What I have to say isn't going to give you grounds to arrest anybody."

Reluctantly I sat down at the table while she opened the oven to check on supper. Pork roast, cabbage, and new potatoes by the looks and smell of it.

She said, "You remember that I said I had a couple leads as to who might have lived in that orphanage?"

"I remember."

Satisfied that supper was doing well, she closed the oven door and sat down across from me. "Adelle Holland was one of those people. . ."

"Who was the other?" I said, unable to wait any longer.

She told me. Then it all made sense.

"How did you find out?" I said.

"You've got Aunt Emma to thank for that. Unknown to

me, she'd been doing some backtracking on her own. She said the man just didn't smell right to her, that he didn't seem to be what he said he was. So she set a couple traps that he fell into."

"She would know, wouldn't she?"

"If anyone would. So armed with that information, she went right to the horse's mouth and asked point-blank."

"Roger Farmer?" I couldn't see even Aunt Emma doing that. Not and live to tell about it.

"Who's Roger Farmer?'

"That's what Howdy Heavin's name used to be."

"No, she went to Howdy's mother, Elizabeth."

"And Elizabeth told her?"

"Howard did. He said he couldn't cover for the boy any longer."

"Excuse me, Ruth. I have to make a phone call."

But Clarkie wasn't home from work yet. And when I tried to call him a few minutes later, his line was busy. Hadn't he ever heard of call waiting?

"You might as well eat your supper," Ruth said as she served it up. "Before it gets cold."

I started to protest that I didn't have time to eat—until I got a good whiff of the pork roast and cabbage. Then I nearly ran over Daisy on my way to the table. Ten minutes later, I was done, which was a new record for me. From there I went right to the phone and was relieved when my call went through.

"Clarkie, this is Garth. I need for you to run a check on somebody for me."

"Who?" he sounded suspicious or at the very least, reluctant.

"Why? Isn't your computer there?"

"It's here." But he didn't volunteer anything more.

"Is it working?"

"Yes. It's working. *Up* is the proper word."

I'd just run out of patience with him. "I don't give a shit what the proper word is, Clarkie. I need some information, and I need it fast. And I'm willing to pay for it if you're too goddamned cheap to do it on your own."

I figured that since he was now a private citizen, so to speak, he was tired of doing free research for people. Either that or he had a hot date that he had to get to. The real reason didn't occur to me until much later, when I got slapped in the face with it.

"I'll be glad to help you out, Garth," he said with that hurt in his voice that I was so used to hearing. "But it might be a while before I can get back to you."

"How long is a while?" Without realizing it, I'd started to drum my fingers on the woodwork.

"I don't know, Garth. Why don't you first tell me what you want to know?"

I told him.

When he answered, he almost sounded relieved. "I'll get on it as soon as I can. I should have something for you tonight."

"I was hoping for sooner, Clarkie."

"I'm sure you were." He hung up.

"Damn," I said, returning to the table where Ruth was just finishing her supper.

"What's wrong?" as if she didn't know.

"I hurt Clarkie's feelings again. You'd think with all of the miles now between us and all of the miles we've logged together, I could at least be civil to him. But I wasn't. And what's worse, I'm not sure I ever can be. How do you explain that to me, Ruth?"

"Ask Karl. He was the same with our son. Karl loved Richard with all of his heart, but up until the day Richard died, the two of them could not speak two words to each other without getting into an argument of some kind."

Richard was Ruth's son, Staff Sergeant Richard Krammes, who had been killed in Vietnam.

"But Clarkie is not my son," I said.

"No. But you treat him like one. And around you, he acts like one. I tell you, Garth, the best thing he ever did was to take that job in Madison. And don't you dare do anything that might bring him back here again."

"Do you think he's working this case on his own?" I hadn't thought of that until now, but the way Clarkie was acting, it was a possibility.

"I wouldn't rule it out, Garth. Why else wouldn't he jump to help you? He has every other time you've asked."

Now, along with feeling like a heel, I felt like a fool. But calling Clarkie back with an apology wasn't the answer. As wired as I was now, I'd only get pissed about something else.

"I hate waiting, Ruth. I'm not a patient person."

"Then help me with the dishes."

One of these days, soon I hoped, I'd learn what my grandfather had tried to teach my father and what he in turn had tried to teach me. "When in doubt, Orrin, keep your mouth shut."

CHAPTER 25

As soon as the last dish was dried and put away, I called Clarkie back to light a fire under him if nothing else. My impatience was rewarded by a busy signal. There was, I decided, justice after all.

Not two minutes after that, Clarkie called me. "I got what you wanted, Garth. You want it in capsule form or all of it?"

"All of it."

It took him about five minutes.

"Where are you going?" Ruth asked, as I strapped on Eugene's holster. It had taken me five more minutes to tell Ruth what Clarkie had told me.

"Doc Airhart's first. Howdy Heavin's second."

"Why Doc Airhart's first?"

"I want some confirmation that Doc knew Howdy for

what he was."

"Why? It won't help your case any."

"No. But it might help me."

"In what way?"

But I was smart enough, in case we ever came to trial, not to try to answer her.

Outside, it felt strange to be walking the streets of Oakalla armed, and in some ways ridiculous. Though a fair shot with a rifle, if I had a rest, I had never learned to shoot a handgun with any accuracy and had only a rudimentary knowledge of the basics involved. But what Clarkie had told me made a weapon seem necessary, and I couldn't very well go armed with a shotgun without attracting more attention than I wanted.

What Clarkie had told me was this: Howdy Heavin had only lasted a month before he went AWOL from the air force. He had never served in Vietnam, never received the Distinguished Flying Cross, never risen to the rank of major, but had by all accounts disappeared off the face of the earth in August 1968. Until a man matching Howdy Heavin's description was arrested on a charge of murder in Rolla, Missouri, in June 1973. The man's name was Roger Farmer. However, before the MPs could arrive in Rolla, Roger Farmer, with the help of a fellow inmate, overpowered a guard and broke jail. His fellow inmate was found dead in a nearby woods. Roger Farmer was still at large.

The back door to Doc's house was unlocked, just as it had always been. I went inside, took a moment to calm myself, then turned on the kitchen light. The sight of Doc's empty kitchen—the table, clock, fan, and chairs, all there without him—hit me where it hurt, and I had to take another moment to reacquaint myself with what I was doing there and why.

It was during that second moment that I heard Doc's

front door open then quietly close. Blinded by the kitchen light, I saw no one, could see no one when I finally made my way outside to Doc's front porch. Howdy Heavin lived across Madison Road just two houses down. There was no comfort in that thought.

Doc's medical files had been searched recently. The searcher had been careful to leave everything in order, but perhaps in his own hurry to leave, he had left Howdy Heavin's file folder sticking a half inch above the others. With my back to the wall, where I could see anyone coming down the hall toward me, I opened Howdy's file and began to read.

Howdy's first five years in Oakalla (medically speaking) had been unremarkable. Along with chicken pox, mumps, and German measles, he'd had a couple bouts with tonsillitis, but no other illnesses to speak of. He had passed a physical his freshman year in high school to play basketball, but since he'd had no more physical examinations after that, it led me to believe that Howdy's basketball career had been a brief one.

It was the psychological examination, given when Howdy was eighteen, and Doc's evaluation of it that got most of my attention. The occasion for the examination was Elizabeth and Howard Heavin's belief that Howdy was the one killing the cats in the south end of Oakalla.

Doc wrote: I do not want to say that the boy is evil, but I can think of no other word to describe him. He seems to have no conscience, not one that I can find anyway, and men without conscience do unconscionable things to the human body, the human spirit, as I witnessed in the long and bloody war of which I was too much a part. But they, those cankers of man's soul, were names without faces, hidden as they were behind their barbed wire, their concentration camps, their pompous goose-stepping army ordained by them to rule the world—hideous caricatures of men rather than man himself. And like a gargoyle high on a roof, they were no threat to me. But this boy has a name and a face, and he lives within a good stone's throw of me. And I fear him. I fear him because he is bad and I have no power to move him toward the good. He is a law unto himself, answering to no higher laws than his own whims, his own powers of deceit. He will not stop killing cats because he does not choose to stop killing cats. No other reason. If he found some pleasure in it, I might understand, and by understanding, help him. But there is no pleasure beyond the simple act of doing it, no rhyme nor reason beyond its opportunity. As Hillary once climbed mountains because they were there, Howdy Heavin kills cats because they are there. It is beyond me. He is beyond me. Beyond us, and I speak of civilization as I know it. Our only hope, as civilized beings, is to do the unthinkable, which is to send him off to war and hope he is killed there. And yet in him, I do not see a future soldier. He is, I think, too much of a coward to ever wear a soldier's stripes, to meet his equal face-to-face. He would much prefer to wait in the shadows and choose his victims from there. And chameleon that he is, he will find shadows everywhere.

Howard and Elizabeth Heavin did not want to answer the knock at their back door. First one, then the other, would rock forward as if about to rise, then settle back down again to rest their arms upon the kitchen table. But perhaps more than a matter of will, it was a matter of inertia, the inability to set their bodies in motion. Life had beaten them down to the point that they just couldn't go any longer.

I went on inside. "Where's Howdy?" I said.

"Gone," Howard answered.

"Gone where?"

"Who knows? Do you know, Elizabeth?" Howard's voice was completely flat, no life at all left in it.

"Somewhere," Elizabeth said in the same dull voice. "He left on foot then came back for his bicycle a few minutes later."

"How long ago?"

"I don't know. Do you, Howard?"

He shrugged. Obviously they hadn't been keeping track of time.

"So you mind if I sit down?" I said. "I have some questions that need answers."

Howdy couldn't get too far away on his bicycle. Besides, I had an idea where he might be going.

Neither Howard nor Elizabeth responded, so I sat down.

"He'll be back," Howard said with conviction. "If we wait long enough. You can ask him your questions."

"I'm not sure I can wait that long. I'm not sure the world can," I said.

"He's no threat to the world. Just to us." Howard looked sadly at Elizabeth, who was looking away. "Isn't that right, Mother?"

But not even that hated word could bring Elizabeth Heavin to life. "That's right, Howard. You're always right, Howard. You told me from the beginning that there was something not quite right about the boy, that the woman at the orphanage let him go too cheap, but no, I wanted a son to carry on the family store, the family name, and the son I wanted was Howdy."

"We couldn't have kids," Howard explained. "And Elizabeth and I were getting along in years and wanted a child of our own, if for nothing else to run the store after we no longer could. We'd tried to adopt, but every place we went kept putting us off, saying maybe next year, knowing all the time that next year would be the same as the last. Then we heard about the orphanage and how some people got kids there fast, no questions asked. So we figured what the heck, it was worth a shot." Howard shook his head in regret. "What a mistake. Our lives were never the same after that. First, we were worried that we wouldn't get our first choice, which was Howdy because he seemed the pick of the litter. Then we were worried about the deal itself, what if, after paying for Howdy, something went wrong and we lost him and our money both. Then once we got him here at home and were certain that we were going to be able to keep him, I began to wonder about the boy himself. First why she was willing to take just five hundred dollars for him when I had heard we might have to pay as much as five thousand. Then why he kept so much to himself and never wanted to play with the other kids in the neighborhood. It was only after Dewey Clinton and his folks moved to town that Howdy had any friends at all. That in itself was a worry to us, why he would choose a feeble-minded boy like Dewey over everybody else."

"Because kids are more perceptive than we give them credit for," Elizabeth said. "They can spot the rotten apple in the barrel long before we can. Unless, like Dewey Clinton, they're too dumb to know better."

"Elizabeth," Howard warned, "we said we weren't going to make any judgments about Howdy."

"You blind old fool!" she shouted. "How can we *not* judge him? He's ruined our store and wrecked our lives and brought his murderous ways home with him to the people we know and love. I'd kill him myself if I had the courage."

Her explosion took the last of Elizabeth Heavin's remaining strength. She had raised her arm to make a fist.

She let her arm drop wearily to the table, bent over to rest her head on it, and wept.

Frozen in place, Howard watched her as he might the end of a sad play, too close to tears himself to offer any comfort.

"It hasn't been easy," he said, "being Howdy's mother."

Or his father either, I imagined.

"When did you realize that there was something seriously wrong with Howdy?" I said.

"That business over the cats. That's when I knew we had real trouble on our hands," Howard said. "Before then, we'd had a few fingers pointed at the south end—you know, nothing really serious, but still cause for concern, like maybe somebody's window being broken, or their trash can tipped over. But that was usually laid at Dewey Clinton's feet, probably because he was such an easy target. The dead cats, though, that was something else again. People were up in arms over that and not just the south end either. Again people were blaming Dewey for it, but Dewey had been in our house enough times by then that I knew him well enough to know he wasn't capable of doing it. There wasn't a mean bone in him."

"Not so with your own son?"

Howard glanced at Elizabeth who was still bent over the table with her head resting on her arm. Occasionally she would sob when her grief got the best of her, but for the most part she cried in silence.

"No. We were on to Howdy's tricks by then," Howard said. "He'd smile and play the innocent, but those eyes of his, cold as they were, told us what was going on."

"How did you discover he was the one killing the cats?"

"Elizabeth found him out. She followed him one night on his rounds. What she saw would turn your stomach."

"That's when you sent him to Doc Airhart?"

Howard nodded. "Howdy didn't want to go, but we told him that if he didn't go, we were sending him back to the orphanage. We wouldn't have, of course," Howard hurried on to explain. "But that was the only leverage we had on the boy. Threats of any other kind went right on by like he hadn't even heard."

"What did Doc have to say about him?"

"On the record or off?" Howard said. "To Elizabeth and me together, he said that he had talked as sternly as he could to Howdy, but he didn't think that the cat killings would stop. . ." Howard's eyes looked inward as he pondered what came next. "But on the way out, Doc pulled me to one side and told me that I'd do the world and myself a favor if I held Howdy's head under the water the next time we went swimming. He'd even help if I needed an extra pair of hands."

"What did you say to that?"

"It made me mad. I told Doc he shouldn't joke about stuff like that."

"He wasn't joking."

"Too late I realized that."

"What finally *did* stop Howdy from killing the cats?" I said.

"He got drafted. Only he joined the air force instead. I tell you, Garth, that was Elizabeth's and my happiest day in six years, the day he reported for duty. Hell of a thing to say about your own son, but it's the truth."

Elizabeth Heavin forced herself to raise her head, then sat stone faced, staring at the kitchen wall. Though too numb to take part, she didn't want Howard to go through this alone.

"Honey, you might as well go on to bed," Howard said.

But she shook her head.

"Had Howdy ever threatened you in any way?" I said.

"Not in so many words. Not even in anything he did. But being around him every day, especially after you crossed him a few times, you got the feeling that you weren't even there as far as he was concerned. You were a means to an end, and once he didn't need you anymore. . ." Howard let that hang. "Well, you can figure it out."

"Why then did you cover for him all of those years he was gone, make up lies that made him seem far better than he was? You had to know what you were doing."

"We did know what we were doing, Garth. We also knew Howdy might come back someday, any day, and he'd want to know what we'd been saying about him in his absence. There's no shame in lying about your kids. People do it all the time whether they know it or not. If not to their neighbors, they do to themselves. We're not alone in that, not by a long shot."

For the first time that evening Howard's voice came to life as he found something to defend. Even Elizabeth found the strength to nod her head in vigorous agreement with him.

"You promoted a deadly lie, Howard. You and Elizabeth both. It ended up getting two good men killed. Not to mention Dewey Clinton, who in your own words didn't have a mean bone in his body."

"Yes. And we'll suffer in hell for it, if that's our fate. But at the time, we thought we had no other choice. Even looking back now, it's still a tough call. No one should have to live in fear of his own life, Garth. Not me, not you, not anybody."

"But have your lies helped anybody? Aren't you still in fear of your own life? Aren't I, because Howdy's path and mine have crossed?"

Howard hung his head, offered nothing in his defense. It was Elizabeth who spoke up. "Then you stop him!" she shouted as she pointed a finger at me. "Mr. All-So-High-

And-Mighty, you stop him. They maybe we'll all get some peace back in our lives."

As I rose from their kitchen table, I felt the weight of Eugene Yuill's gun on my hip.

CHAPTER 26

My first stop after leaving Howard and Elizabeth Heavin was Eugene Yuill's house. There his patrol car still sat parked in his driveway, but tonight the driver's side door was unlocked and Eugene's missing keys were in the ignition. As I slipped in behind the wheel and tried without success to start the car, as Howdy Heavin evidently had done earlier that night, I silently thanked Danny Palmer for his person and his skill.

My second stop was at the Marathon to pick up Jessie. She didn't want to start, but she finally did after I had pumped a hole in the floor where her accelerator used to be. Her fuel pump was probably going out. Besides her engine itself, it was about the only thing I hadn't replaced on her.

The drive north on Fair Haven Road, then east on

Haggerty Lane, could have been a pleasant one had I been in the right frame of mind to enjoy it. The night was warm, the moon and stars were out, the air had a country sweetness about it that had started at the edge of town. For her, Jessie was running well. For me, I was unusually calm, and that was the crux of my problem.

Ordinarily I would have been more alert to, more aware of what was going on inside me. But I was numb inside, as if everything in there had shut down, and I could no longer think, only act and react.

As an athlete, I had occasionally gotten into a zone, sometimes when pitching baseball or playing basketball, but more often when running the half mile, when everything else within and without me dissolved into the act itself, and the only feeling, if there was one, was that of exhilaration, the seemingly effortless flow of my muscles as part of some all-consuming tide. Which of course was a lie. So fully focused was I that I chose not to feel my own pain and only later discovered that I had pushed myself beyond my limits, and it hurt.

That force was operating in me now, had me by the throat and wouldn't let go. But there was nothing free flowing or artistic about it. Not even close. What had mastered and at the same time empowered me was the primitive thirst for revenge. I wanted Howdy Heavin's head. It was as simple as that.

Nothing stirred in the orphanage. No birds fluttered nervously as I approached it. No resident coons crawled in or out of its windows or quarreled over who would be sleeping where tonight. No evidence of any human occupants either. But I would have bet this month's mortgage payment that Howdy Heavin was in there somewhere.

I had brought the flashlight from Jessie's glove compartment, and like Jessie, it was a slow starter, but once I'd warmed it up, I could now switch it on and off with ease. So intent was I on Howdy Heavin that it never occurred to me that he might have an accomplice until I was halfway up the back stairs of the orphanage when stopping to catch my breath, I heard someone on the stairs below me. Or maybe, instead of an accomplice, it was Howdy himself.

The prudent act was to go back down the stairs to find out. So I did—with Eugene's .38 Police Special cocked and held in both hands at the ready-fire position. But it was hard to be quiet on a stairs littered with dead leaves and wasp nests. When I reached the bottom of the stairs again, no one was there.

"I know you're out there," I said quietly. "But this is between Howdy and me. So if you're smart, you'll stay out of it."

But I saw no one move to challenge me, heard no words of rebuttal. I took that as my answer and without wasting any more time, hurried back up the stairs. Let his accomplice come. Once I had Howdy in my sights, I really didn't care what happened next.

But it proved all too easy. I charged into the third-floor dormitory, turned on my flashlight, and before it could even sweep the room once, its beam fell upon Howdy Heavin. He didn't seem to be surprised. Not at all. In fact, he seemed to welcome the company.

"Good evening, Garth. I've been expecting you," he said.

Dressed for the night in dark jeans and a navy pullover sweatshirt, Howdy also wore black tennis shoes and a look of utter control that made me wonder just what was going on.

"It is Garth, isn't it?" He sounded as if he'd be disappointed if it weren't.

"It's me."

"I thought it was. And you've come to kill me, right?"

"Right after I get some answers."

Howdy stood facing the light with his left hand casually resting on an iron bed. If it were a pose, it was an impressive one.

"Why should I bother with answers if you're going to kill me anyway?"

"Because I'll hurt you before I kill you."

Howdy's hand closed a little tighter around the bed. For the first time, I smelled fear on him.

"You wouldn't do that," he said. "It's not your style."

I was tempted to shoot him in the kneecap just to wipe the smile off his face, but that would require more skill than I had. I shot at the iron bed instead, hitting the one next to it. As the sparks flew, Howdy instinctively ducked away from them. That gave me my chance to close the gap between us.

"I don't think I can miss from here," I said, aiming at his groin.

A muscle in his face began to twitch. I didn't know whether it was from hate or fear.

"Put away the gun," Howdy said. "Then I'll tell you what you want to know."

"Sit down on the floor, Howdy. Then *I'll* tell *you* what I want to know. Now! Goddamn you!" I yelled when he hesitated.

He sat down on the floor. I lowered Eugene's gun and let it rest against my right leg. At first quarter, the moon's light was streaming in the south window. When I was sure that I could make Howdy out in the dark, I shut off the flashlight.

"Speak, Howdy," I said.

"Where do you want me to start?"

"With James Garmone. Why did you kill him?"

"I didn't kill him. Dewey did."

I raised Eugene's .38 Police Special until Howdy was looking directly into the bore of it. I said, "Your one chance, Howdy, is to tell me the truth. Then you might live to see a judge and jury. Otherwise, you won't."

"You're not God, Garth. You don't have the right to judge me."

"Maybe not, Howdy. But I do have an overwhelming urge to kill you. And at this particular moment, that's all that matters."

Perhaps he saw that I was serious. Perhaps he found a new angle to play. At any rate, Howdy decided to talk.

"I didn't intend to kill James Garmone," he said. "At least that's not the way it started out. At first, all Buddy and I wanted from him was a couple smokes."

"Buddy Brewer?"

"Yes. Buddy Brewer. How did you know?"

"Adelle Holland told me."

A change came over Howdy. There was no mistaking his look now, which was one of hatred.

"Miss Holland. The witch woman herself. I thought she'd be dead by now."

"No such luck, Howdy. She's alive and well in White Lake."

In the silence that followed, I could almost see his mind at work. And the vision was frightening to behold.

"Perhaps one of the stops I should have made," he said. "I've been in every state, you know, except Hawaii."

"Why not Hawaii?"

He shrugged. He didn't have a reason.

"And left a body in every one?"

"Not as many as you might think, Garth."

"How many, Howdy?"

Again he shrugged. "I lost count a long time ago."

Seeing Howdy Heavin up close, I found that it was harder to hate him than it was from a distance. In his jeans and sweatshirt, with his hard lean body, close-cropped hair, and trim red mustache, he looked like the former air force officer he had professed to be. Not even his eyes gave him away. Intense, at once playful and curious, they didn't seem the eyes of a madman but those of a willful child.

"Having second thoughts?" Howdy said. Howdy knew how to read people, which was part of his genius, and all of his terror.

"No, Howdy. Not second thoughts. Only troubled ones. Why did you kill James Garmone?"

Howdy studied me a moment longer, then, smiling, looked away. Whatever he was looking for in me, apparently he had found.

"As I said, Buddy and I just wanted to hit the professor up for smokes, like we had before. Except he was down to his last two, and besides that, we were too young to be smoking anyway, so he said no, we couldn't have any. Buddy said to me, let's go. We'll go back into the woods and smoke some grapevine, which is what we did when we couldn't get cigarettes. I said no, I had a better idea. Because right about then Dewey had come along, and I knew he'd do about anything I told him. First, I said, we were going to have some fun at the professor's expense. So I told Dewey what I wanted him to do, and then Buddy and I hid along the creek where we'd have a good view of it."

"You told Dewey to drop a rock on James Garmone's head?" Which, I was certain, was what he had told Dewey to do to me.

"No. You had to know how Dewey's mind worked. I told Dewey that the professor was a bad man and needed to be taught a lesson. Dewey took it from there. He broke a piece of slate right over the professor's head."

"And you did the rest?"

"I had to because of Buddy. He got up to run away, and the professor saw us. I'll never forget that as long as I live. There he stood in the water—dazed, not knowing what happened or even where he was, glasses hanging from one ear, hat smashed down over his ears—and looking right at me, as if he knew I were to blame for it all. I shoved Buddy aside and went after him."

"You drowned him yourself?"

"I had to. Buddy was of no help to me, and Dewey had lit out for parts unknown." Howdy paused as he relived it again. "Later, back at the orphanage, I told myself that it was really self-defense, that I wasn't such a monster after all. Except, and I've always remembered this, too, even while I was holding the professor's head under water, I was taking those two cigarettes out of his shirt pocket." He smiled then shrugged. "Now I don't even smoke."

"Except for some grapevine with Dewey."

He was surprised that I knew. "You don't miss much, do you?"

"I try not to."

"The funny thing is that even though the professor was a lot stronger than I was, he didn't put up much of a fight for his life. A lot of people don't. I think they're too shocked by the fact that it's even happening."

I didn't know enough about that to comment. But perhaps Howdy was right. Who among us ever expects to be murdered?

"What happened then?"

"We heard somebody coming down the road, so we headed for the woods, thinking that Dewey had done the same. Then when he turned up awhile later, I told him he'd done it now, he'd killed the professor."

"Were you hoping that he would then throw himself

off of Wildwood Bridge?"

"I could only hope for that, which at the time seemed the perfect solution. But I'm glad it didn't happen. Dewey turned out to be the only real friend I ever had."

I was surprised by the tears in his eyes. They couldn't have been for Dewey. They had to be for Howdy.

"Are you the one who dragged James Garmone's body back into the middle of the creek?" After Shank Doyle had dragged it out.

"Dewey and I did. Buddy wanted nothing more to do with it. Then I told Dewey that he mustn't tell anyone what had happened because it would get us all in trouble, and he might never see me again. Poor Dewey," he said. "I know he tried, but that was asking too much of him. Not only did he tell, he tried to take the blame for it."

"And nearly succeeded," I said.

"Yeah, I know," Howdy said. "I read Doc's memoirs." Howdy seemed more troubled by Dewey's action than I thought he would have been. But then I was the last person to ask how Howdy Heavin's mind worked.

"Where are Doc's memoirs?" I said.

He shook his head. He didn't know. "I left them on Dewey's kitchen table."

"Before or after you killed the cat?"

"Before. Killing the cat wasn't part of the plan. But there it was, rubbing against me, wanting to be fed, with Dewey in the next room, hanging by his clothesline. What kind of loyalty was that?"

I studied Howdy Heavin for even the trace of a smile. Surely even he could see the irony in that statement. But apparently he didn't.

"Why did Buddy have to die?" I said.

"Buddy was a pain in the ass, that's why. In the first place, I knew I couldn't trust him to keep his mouth shut.

In the second place, he threatened to tell Witch Holland what I'd done if I didn't agree to have Mother and Dad adopt him, too, which they never would have done because Witch Holland would have wanted too much for him. I didn't want him messing things up for me, not my one chance to get out of there. So that next night, I held a pillow over his face, then slid him down the fire escape. The whole thing was a lot easier than I ever thought it would be."

"The killing itself or getting away with it?"

"Both."

"And that's when you discovered you liked killing?"

"That's when I discovered it didn't bother me to kill. There's a difference."

I listened to a sudden gust of wind shake the trees outside, the barrage of leaves as they struck the roof of the orphanage, then skidded across it to the ground. A change in the weather was on the way. The wind never blew just to amuse itself.

Then in the lull that followed, I heard floorboards creak. Somewhere in the belly of the orphanage, something was on the prowl.

But either Howdy didn't hear it or he chose to ignore it. He was more intent on me.

"So to cover up one killing, you killed again?" I said.

"That's the way it sometimes happens. But I almost didn't get away with it, and wouldn't have gotten away with it, if Witch Holland hadn't been so anxious to get rid of me. Doc Airhart was one smart man, I'll grant him that. By leaving Buddy's body in Pine Creek, I had fooled everybody but him."

"Is that why you killed Doc?"

"His memoirs were coming out, Garth. Nineteen sixty-two. I couldn't afford to let that happen."

"And Eugene Yuill?"

"An accident. I never intended to draw attention to myself by killing Eugene. And had I been less lazy, it never would have happened."

"By going out the front door instead of the back?" I was guessing.

"By going down Fickle Road instead of Madison Road. I looked around, saw no one there, and decided to save myself a few steps by going directly home, instead of circling in. The minute I hit the sidewalk in front of Doc's house, Eugene's lights went on. He had been parked in a shadow in the alley across the street."

From then on I knew what had happened. But I wanted Howdy's version of it, no matter how much it hurt.

"So how did you get Eugene out of his car and his night stick in your hand?"

"By asking him to show it to me, which he was only too eager to do. I was leaning in his window, shooting the shit, when I asked him about it, and he handed it over to me. Then I turned around, holding it up to the streetlight so that I could get a better look at it, when my eyes fell on his back tire. 'Eugene,' I said, 'I think you've got a tire going flat.' He was out of the car in a flash. I'd never seen Eugene move so fast. And when he knelt down for a better look, I hit him. Then again and again, when he tried to rise."

Howdy spoke throughout it all in the same matter-of-fact voice. As Doc had noted long ago and as Howdy had just confirmed, he took no pleasure in killing. For him, it was a reflex action, as casual as wiping his nose.

"Then you drove Eugene out here, buried him, then dug him up again the night that Dewey hanged himself?"

"That's pretty much the order," Howdy said. "Once you found Eugene's grave, I knew I had to act fast."

"Where were you when I was down there, up here at

the window?" Which was where I felt he was.

"No. We were hiding in the woods the whole time. We had our bicycles along, remember?"

Howdy's answer wrung out a cold drop of sweat that slowly rolled down my spine. If not Howdy, who was up here looking down at me?

"But you had been up here earlier, smoking grapevine and sliding down the fire escape?"

"Not that day we hadn't."

The bead of sweat continued across my rump and down my right leg. I'd figure it out later, I hoped.

"So you sicced Dewey on me then had to cover your tracks when he missed me with the rock."

"Dewey never could get things right. I told him that you had to die because you were going to put us both in jail otherwise. Besides, it was all his fault for getting me in this mess in the first place. If he hadn't killed the professor, I wouldn't be in trouble now." Howdy was still angry at Dewey, and it showed. "I can't tell you how furious I was when he rode up and said he'd missed. How could he? I yelled. He hung his head and said he didn't know, he just did."

I knew or thought I did. All of Howdy's bullying couldn't override Dewey's essential goodness. He had chosen to miss me on purpose then ended up dying because of it.

"How did you get Dewey to bury Eugene Yuill?" I said.

"Not only did I get him to bury him, but I had him dig Eugene up, then leave his fingerprints all over Eugene's night stick. I told Dewey he owed me that much, for messing up my life the way he had."

"It seems the other way around."

Again, Howdy didn't see the irony. "Not to him, it didn't."

"You felt no remorse at all for having your only true friend kill himself for you?"

"It bothered me, sure. But you have to realize it was either him or me. It's a choice we all have to make at one time or another."

At last I saw to the bottom of Howdy Heavin's soul. It wasn't hard because his life, his deeds were a perfect mirror of it. Everything else that might be said about him was only so much bullshit.

But then what did I do with that knowledge? Shoot him down as the mad dog I knew him to be? A half-hour ago I could have done that with ease. Now, I wasn't so sure. And what bothered me even more was that Howdy Heavin knew that.

I said, "You were the one who came into my office and went through my files the day of Doc's funeral. How did you manage that and still get your name on the list?"

"I told Mother and Dad to put it there." He smiled. "They usually do what I say."

"But then Pete Nelson and Milo Thomas came and nearly caught you in the act?"

"Yes. I'd already found what I wanted and was on my way out when here they came. I didn't have time to close the door. The best I could do was to go out the front door while they were coming in the back."

"Then you went to Doc's house and took a rubber hose to Daisy."

"She wouldn't let me into the basement, which was where I wanted to go. I knew from Doc's memoirs that Buddy's body had been found, but there was no account of it in the newspaper, so that meant it had to be around somewhere. Without his body, there was nothing to tie me to his murder. But that damn dog ruined everything."

"She probably remembered you from before."

"Before?"

"The night you killed Doc."

"Dogs aren't that smart."

I was starting to think that this one was.

"Why, Howdy?"

I was down to my last question. But as usual, I'd run out of answers before I'd run out of questions.

"Why do I kill people? I'll give you the same answer I gave Doc when he asked about the cats. I don't know."

"No. Why did you ever come here to Oakalla, and why did you ever come back?"

"That's easy. I came here because I was sick of living in the orphanage. I came back because it was home."

Home? I never thought that word would leave me cold.

"Then what are you doing here in the orphanage now?" One more question couldn't hurt, since I didn't yet know what to do with Howdy Heavin.

"Remembering, Garth. What it's like to be a nobody." He rose and dusted himself off. "No more questions?"

"No. No more questions."

"Then I'll be going."

I pointed Eugene's revolver at him. "I can't let you do that, Howdy."

"Of course you can, Garth," he said while casually taking a step backwards that effectively put him out of my reach. "Doc Airhart let me go on, and he knew what I was. So did the air force, my parents, and dozens of other people I could name. So did Witch Holland, who was the first to know me for what I was. They let me out of their lives in the hope that I would never walk back in. Why? For most of them, like my folks, it was easier that way. And safer, too, they figured. For Doc, as it is for you, it was a matter of principle. No matter what he thought of me, he couldn't kill me. Not in cold blood. Neither, I'm willing to bet, can you." He slipped another step away from me.

"You've seen his file on you, then?" I said, trying to

distract him from his purpose, which was escape.

"No. I never have. But I could read his eyes just like I can read yours. I knew what he thought of me, what he wished for me, but it never happened."

Eugene's gun had grown slick in my hand. I brought my left hand up to my right to help hold it. Now that I most needed my concentration, that single-minded intent of purpose that I had brought with me into the orphanage, I had lost it. Like the leaves rushing across the roof, thoughts were going too fast to track. Not cold blood. Self-defense. My self-defense, Abby's, Ruth's, and the rest of Oakalla. All good people everywhere who deserved not to walk in fear. But would the grand jury see it that way? Or some judge in Madison who never knew Howdy Heavin? And what about the badge in my wallet? I was the law in Oakalla, damn it, whether I liked it or not. And what would that law be worth once I pulled the trigger on Howdy Heavin?

"I thought you'd see it my way," Howdy said, as he edged ever nearer to the fire escape. A couple more steps and he could make a dive for it.

Then a figure in the doorway momentarily distracted me. When I looked again, Howdy had already made his move.

The blast from the shotgun nearly cut Howdy Heavin in two and had the effect of making my own shot go wild. Though in truth, I probably would have missed anyway.

My next brief close-up look at Howdy was not what made me run down the back stairs. Neither was I in pursuit of the one who had shot him. Already I knew who it was, had glimpsed his face in the fire of the muzzle blast.

No, it was the other face I had seen. When rising after examining Howdy's body, I had felt someone else's presence there in the room with me and chanced a look over my shoulder. There at the window was the apparition of a boy. Or so it seemed at the time. Since, I have wondered if it wasn't the lingering glow of the muzzle blast—and my own fertile imagination.

Jessie waited there in the moonlight, ready to take me home. Or such was my delusion. I had forgotten that she didn't need to wait until midnight to turn into a pumpkin or in this case, have her fuel pump go the rest of the way out. With a curse, I slammed her door and started the long walk back to town.

CHAPTER 27

Ruth and I were the first ones up the next morning. I didn't know her excuse, but I had yet to go to bed.

After a somewhat subdued homecoming, during which I had soaked my aching feet while telling Ruth and Abby how the evening had gone, I had called the Wisconsin State Police and then had to accompany their investigators back out to the orphanage and what they described as "the scene of the crime." Howdy Heavin being the victim and all.

They found both of the slugs from Eugene's .38 imbedded in the walls of the dormitory, so they couldn't very well blame Howdy's demise on me. As for Howdy's "unknown assailant," as he would later be described by the Madison media, he had made a clean getaway, leaving not one shred of evidence behind. Then I told the officer in charge that, based on my best instincts, they would have a better shot at the Abominable Snowman than they would at catching him. A bright man, he said that, under the circumstances, his best instincts told him the same thing.

When we arrived back in Oakalla, he let me off at my office where I stayed until I was too bleary eyed to see anymore. Then I walked home, arriving just as Ruth was coming down the stairs to put the coffee on.

While she poured the coffee, I found some week-old donuts in the cupboard and set them on the table. I didn't have time for breakfast, but the donuts would at least take my mind off it.

"Is Abby heading home today?" Ruth asked.

"She says she is."

From my office, I had called to tell Abby good night and ended up talking for a half-hour. Then, though we had run out of things to say, neither of us wanted to get off the phone.

"That's too bad. I've liked having her here," Ruth said.

"I have, too." More than Ruth would ever know.

"Is she still headed for Detroit?"

"Unless she's told you different."

Ruth shook her head no. "What about Daisy?" Who now had her eye on Ruth, whom, though she denied it, I suspected of upping the ante as far as Daisy's daily ration of table scraps went.

"Abby said that we would talk about that later."

"Be a shame to stick that dog in a kennel."

"I don't think that's going to happen, Ruth, under any circumstance."

I had time to drink a cup of coffee and put away a couple donuts before Abby came down the stairs, lugging that U-Haul she passed off as her suitcase. "This is adding insult to injury," I said as I carried it to her car.

"Ride with me a ways?" she said.

"You're not staying for coffee?"

"I don't think that would be wise."

"Say good-bye to Ruth at least."

"We said our good-byes last night."

Oh well. . .

The first thing that Daisy did when she got home was to head for Doc's bedroom at full speed, only to return at a slow puzzled walk a couple minutes later. Abby and I stood in the kitchen holding each other. She was crying. I was trying not to.

"We still have almost three months. I don't know why I'm acting like this," she said.

"Maybe part of it's relief."

"Relief over *what?* I feel like somebody has both hands on my heart and is slowly tearing it in two."

"Relief that Doc's murderer is dead. Relief that at last a decision has been made and you can now get on with your life."

She pushed us apart to look at me. "For a smart man, you don't know women very well."

"I've never pretended to."

Then she pulled me against her again. "Thank God for one small favor. I don't think I could stand it if you knew me any better."

"Are you going to be okay?" I asked.

"Is that your subtle way of saying you're leaving?"

"I do have a deadline coming up."

"So do we."

"Yes. But mine's today."

She released me. "Well, I guess I'll let you go, then."

So I went.

The day had turned out about as I expected—cold,

windy, and grey. Spits of rain as hard as BBs pelted me all the way to the far southeast end of town where I found Rupert Roberts in his garage, putting the tarp on his trailer for its trip to Texas.

"Give me a hand?" he said, as he threw me one of the tie ropes.

I secured my end the best I could, then threw the rope back over to him. A failure as a Boy Scout, I had only a passing acquaintance with knots.

"You getting ready to leave?" I said.

"Within the hour, or whenever you get out of here, whichever comes first." He threw the rope back my way.

"I won't keep you long," I said as I ran the rope through an eyelet in the tarp and passed it under the trailer to him. If the tarp held past Oakalla's city limits, I'd be surprised.

What I had come to realize was that the person whose car tracks that Abby and I had found on Milo Thomas's farm, the figure that I had seen leaving Dewey Clinton's yard the day of Dewey's death, the one who had beaten me to Howdy Heavin's medical file and every other step of the way was the same one whose face I had glimpsed last night in the fire of his shotgun. So today I had come to him, feeling both humble and grateful.

"What tipped you off to Howdy?" I said.

"Aunt Emma. She said she thought he bore watching." He was busy fastening the rope to the frame of the trailer.

"Why didn't she tell *me* that?"

"She figured you'd only get in my way."

"I'll have to remember to thank her the next time I see her."

He'd run out of rope, so he went after another one at the back of the garage. Normally at this time of the morning, he and Elvira would have been on their way.

"How did you go the rest of the way with it?" I asked on his return.

"On my own, with a little help from Clarkie. Contrary to what some people think, I used to be a pretty good lawman, even before you arrived on the scene."

"What little help from Clarkie?" I said, ignoring the barb aimed at me. "Was that you on the phone with him last night?"

"Which time?"

Shit, I thought. No wonder Clarkie was so hesitant to help me, since he was already committed to helping Rupert.

"It looks like I owe Clarkie another apology," I said.

He tossed me the other rope. "It appears you do."

"And the shotgun?" I said.

"A ten-gauge that belonged to my father. It used to be his goose gun, though I don't remember him ever shooting a goose with it. He left me a box of number 2 magnums to go with it. I guess it pays to keep your powder dry."

The rope was in my hand, but I had yet to do anything with it. "Where might the shotgun not be found now?"

"The bottom of Hidden Quarry." Which was over two hundred feet deep in some places.

"A good place for it."

"That's what I figured."

Then he cleared his throat. I got the message and got busy with the rope.

"You realize that I can't tie a knot worth a damn," I said. "I can't guarantee you'll even get out of the driveway with this."

"I'll take my chances." Then he reached under the tarp and brought out a grocery sack tied in a bundle. "Here," he said, handing it across the trailer to me. "I planned to mail it to you if you didn't get here by this morning."

"Doc's memoirs?"

"Yes."

"After last night, I figured you had them. Where were you parked anyway?"

"Milo Thomas's place. The same place I'd parked before."

"We seem to have covered a lot of the same ground."

"And probably always will."

He smiled at me. It made me feel about ten feet tall.

"What was in here that Howdy Heavin was so afraid of?" I asked as I untied the sack.

"Nothing as I found them on Dewey's kitchen table. Everything in there pointed to Dewey. It was the page that I found under Howdy's mattress that let the cat out of the bag, so to speak. It's on top in there if you care to read it."

It said: And when Dewey led me to the second body there below the bridge, I was more convinced than ever that this poor addled child had indeed "done it," as he claimed. It wasn't until later, when I discovered no water in the boy's lungs, that I began to have my doubts. . .

There was more. But I'd have time to read it later. I retied the sack and stuck it under my arm, as I prepared to leave.

"Take care of yourself," I said, offering my hand across the trailer. "It could get nasty."

Rupert shook my hand. I loved his grip. Dry, firm, and sure, it let me know that there were still some things in life left to hold on to.

"I'm going south, remember?" he said.

"It never snows in Texas?"

"Not very often where we are."

It was time for me to leave, but I still had something left to say. "Thanks for last night. I'm not sure I could have pulled the trigger on Howdy Heavin."

"You would have been justified, Garth. He was a fleeing

felon."

"I'm not sure that the powers that be would have looked at it that way."

"You might be right."

I started to leave. His voice stopped me.

"But now you understand why that badge gets heavy sometimes," he said. "Why it's easier on me with it off."

"And harder on me with it on?"

"What goes around, comes around."

I smiled as I remembered our early years together, how frustrated he would get at me when I would bend the rules, how frustrated I would get at him because he wouldn't. Now that the shoe was on the other foot, I would have traded places with him in a second.

"How right you are," I said.

"Don't let it get you down."

A shrug was my answer. I couldn't let him know that it already had.

The rain was in my face all the way back to my office. But in a sense, I welcomed it because it gave me something to rail at.

Once at my office, I tried to gather my thoughts and focus them on the work ahead. Only sixteen more hours to go and counting . . .

But my mind kept straying to the week just passed. The week that Oakalla lost its grand old man and then two other good men within days of each other. The week that Abby came to stay at my house, and I spent my first full night at hers. The week that I perhaps had glimpsed my first ghost ever, and surely felt its presence; one that saw Ruth saving table scraps, Daisy save the basement, and Rupert save my bacon. A kaleidoscope of brilliant color, intense struggle, and profound sadness, it would go down in my memory book as the week that was.

But the one image that I would cling to, or rather would cling to me, because when distilled, it was the essence of that week, was that on the day we buried Doc, there was snow on the roses.